One Date

Editing by: Allie Bliss from Blissed Out Editing
Proofreading by Sarah Baker from Word Emporium

One Date

KA JAMES

KALEIDOSCOPE PUBLISHING LTD

Blurb

Over the years, Jack O'Riley has shown zero interest in me aside from our friendship. Even when I tried to tell him how I felt four years ago...

That's how I ended up dating his best friend, but now three years later, that's over and Jack's following me on a London sidewalk, asking me for just one date.

I mean, what's the worst that could happen?

The heat in his eyes and the way I've always felt 'seen' by him, has me agreeing, even when I know I should say no.

But then our one date leads to more and to protect myself I say something that's not true. After all, what can a woman like me offer a man who has everything?

Dedication

To anyone who has ever felt like they weren't good enough for another person...

You are more than enough.

Trigger Warnings

To help you decide if this book is for you, I have included a trope and trigger warning outline below. Rest assured, there is a happy ending but to make it interesting for you, there has to be some turbulence on the journey.

This is a contemporary romance.

Tropes: Second Chance, Best Friends Ex, Friends to Lovers, Billionaire

Triggers: Mention of Parental Death

Playlist

Listen Here

Hello - Beyonce
Out Of Reach - Gabrielle
The Night We Met - Lord Huron
JEANS (with Miguel) - Jessie Reyes
All I Ask - Adele
Wondering Why - The Red Clay Strays

Prologue — Sutton

"Don't let him slip away again, Sutton. If you like the guy, just go for it."

As if it's that easy, Minnie.

Jack O'Riley is a friend, first and foremost. Yes, he's the only man to have 'seen' me in the three years we were at college, but during that time, he never once gave me any indication that he was interested in more. That I was a girl he'd date. I have nothing to offer him that he can't already do for himself.

All I have to do is look at the girls he dated, their brilliance bolstering his own, and then everything he's accomplished in the time since we last saw each other.

"What's holding you back, Sutton?"

Everything and nothing.

How do I even answer that question without sounding like some lost teenager afraid to go after her first crush? Of course, that's not what I am. I wouldn't be in the back of this cab if I was. Minnie wouldn't understand where I'm coming from. Not when she can stand on her own two feet, taking on the world so effortlessly, as if her parentage has nothing to do with her position in our circles.

I move my phone to the other ear as the cab crawls along the city roads. There's always been something about Jack that has drawn me to him. Like a moth to a flame or a bee to pollen. I've craved his company since the moment I met him. Butterflies take up residence in the pit of my stomach at the mere thought of him. Even now, I feel... energized at the prospect of seeing him again.

While I was busy, lost in the experience of finally running my own life, adjusting to school, and desperately ignoring my growing feelings for him, he was nothing but kind and sweet. Someone I could confide in and show my true self to as I fumbled my way through the discovery.

It's part of the reason we drifted apart after college. He took his ambition and smarts and made something of himself all on his own. And while I'm successful in my own right, I'm very much aware of the fact that I probably wouldn't have been without my parents' connections.

There was no way I could be around Jack as he bloomed into the successful, self-made man I knew he was supposed to be. The man he's become. Not when my success isn't my own. He needed a woman by his side who matched his brilliance, pushing him while chasing her own passions. Someone with a lot more to offer than I can.

The realization is like a heavy, dark cloud on my mood. Tapping a soothing rhythm on my thigh, I try to lift it, not wanting to have the old doubts on my mind, especially when tonight is about me putting myself out there and getting the guy. It's so easy to get back into the self doubting mindset when thinking back over all the years I've wasted pining for him.

Minnie's voice pulls me back to the conversation. "Do you want to hear my thoughts on the matter?"

Distracted, I reply, "No, but I'm sure you'll tell me anyway."

Her throaty laugh has a smile stretching across my face. "I think the only thing holding you back... is you, Sutton. Tonight, I want you to grab him by the balls, metaphorically, of course—unless he's into that—and make him see what he's missing when it comes to you. What's that quote your favorite teacher used to spout all the time?"

We say it in unison, the memories of Mrs. Wallin standing at the front of the lecture theater rushing back. "You miss one hundred percent of the chances you don't take."

With an excitement I wish could be transferred over the phone, Minnie exclaims, "Exactly! Now go get him, honey, and if he's stupid enough to reject you, I have the perfect man for you."

The cab driver coughs as he pulls the car up to the curb outside the restaurant Jack suggested we meet at. I hand him some bills, telling him to keep the change before I climb out onto the sidewalk. "I'm here," I say to Minnie.

"Okay, so what's the plan?"

Pulling in a reassuring breath, I answer, "Go in there, tell him how I feel, and either walk out with him or my head held high."

"Yes! It's totally going to be with him, darling. I can feel it in my bones."

I laugh, because it's just typical of Minnie to be so dramatic. *Still, I hope she's right.* "As much as I love talking to you, I'm sure you have a cabana boy to seduce and I have a Jack to bare my soul to."

Minnie ignores my teasing comment, instead doing what she does best and cheering me on. "Go get him, girl."

We say goodbye, and with my phone securely in my purse, I smooth my palms over my thighs. Sucking in a deep breath, I will the nerves that seem to have taken up root in the pit of my stomach to calm down. So what if tonight is the first time I've seen Jack O'Riley since we finished college?

It's not a big deal.

Okay, that's a lie. It is a big deal.

Especially when he invited me personally and sounded so happy to hear from me. It's been six long years, and a lot has changed. I've changed a lot since then *and* made something of myself on my own.

Maybe, just maybe, the one-sided crush I had on him all those years ago is finally going to lead somewhere. *No, not maybe.* Christ, I'm a twenty-seven-year-old woman. I am more than capable of asking a guy out.

I've got my favorite lucky little black dress on that clings to my body like a second skin. I'm waxed from the neck down and I've got a perfume on that cost more than most people spend on rent a month. The lady in the store said something about pheromones and attraction... I was sold at the idea of bringing him to his knees. I even went to the hair salon today and got a blowout, so my hair looks its best. Nothing is going to stop me from getting the man.

I pull open the heavy restaurant door and step into the air-conditioned space. It's mid-May and in four weeks I'll be off to the Hamptons to spend some girl time with my friends. So, if everything does go horribly wrong, at least I'll be able to escape the city for a while.

No, Sutton, stop thinking like that.

Jack and I get along, and even if he doesn't feel the same way, we can still be friends. It's all going to be okay because I know that Jack would refuse to let me feel bad about making a pass at him. I can just imagine the easy smile on his handsome face and the feel of his arm as he'd pull me into his side. If nothing else, he'd let me down gently. That thought alone gives me *some* comfort.

With a smile on my lips that feels far too fake, I walk

to the hostess stand, willing the churning in my stomach to subside.

"Hi, I'm meeting Jack O'Riley."

"Of course, they have the back room booked out."

My brows tug together at her remark. *They? Did Jack bring someone?* He didn't mention that he was seeing anyone. Before I even thought about reaching out to him, I practically stalked his social media. A glass of wine too many and I was scouring his accounts for what he'd been up to in the years since college—A lot if the parties and traveling were anything to go by.

But they were pretty sparse the last couple of years.

The start of a headache makes itself known as I follow the hostess through the busy restaurant to a door at the opposite end of the room. She stands back, directing me with her arm and a polite smile, completely unfazed by my dazed and confused stare.

Lifting my delicate gold necklace, I fiddle with it, seeking comfort in the action before I pull in a reassuring breath and push through the door.

My first thought is this can't be right, but as I turn to find the hostess, my eyes land on Jack. My second thought is that *I've* made a mistake. The room is filled with people chatting around a long table. This is a party.

I shouldn't have called him.

I need to leave... now.

Jack lifts his head, his beautiful blue gaze landing on me before an easy lopsided smile lifts the corner of his mouth. My body shuts down and I'm frozen as heat engulfs me. It's like I've been transported back to college and the first time we met. Nobody has ever had control over my body like Jack does. Worst of all, he doesn't even know it.

Somebody walks between us, cutting the intense eye contact. I drop my eyes to the floor and suck in a discreet lungful of air. When I raise them again, Jack's talking to somebody else, oblivious to the moment. The thought that he didn't feel anything hurts, and for a split second I consider turning around and leaving.

It's got to be a sign, right?

We shared a moment, and he felt nothing, so why would I open up to him about wanting to give us a try?

I must be a glutton for punishment because instead of leaving, I find my feet carrying me in the direction of the bar, in desperate need of a strong drink.

I can't believe I was stupid enough to think we would be having an intimate dinner. That fact that I thought he'd take *me* to one of the most exclusive restaurants in the city is almost laughable.

Closing my eyes, I lean against the bar and get my bearings. I replay the conversation we had on Wednesday. Jack definitely didn't say anything about a party. If he had, I'd have asked to meet him alone.

I don't need an audience for my embarrassment. In fact, I should go. I can call him tomorrow and say something came up.

"What can I get you?"

Lifting my head, I give the bartender a weak smile. "A Manhattan, please."

One drink and then I'll leave. Maybe I'll pick up a bottle of wine on the way, get into the tub, and look out over the city as I contemplate my life. Something has to change. I can't keep pining after this man.

A cocktail glass filled with amber liquid is placed in front of me. I snatch it up, taking a hefty swig of the dry and spicy drink. It packs a punch; the alcohol going to my head. *I should have eaten before I left.*

Blowing out a breath, I turn to face the room, scanning it for a quiet corner to have my drink in. Several familiar faces fill my vision. Big names in my father's circle and not people I would expect Jack to be hosting. But what do I know? It's been years and a lot can change in that time.

My brows tug together when two guys walk past me talking about microprocessors and something else I'm not sure of. It sounds like a whole other language and my stomach quivers with unease. *I shouldn't have come.*

Dipping my head, I step away from the bar, walking around the edge of the room. *Be seen not heard, Sutton.* My mother's words echo in my ears, making me lift my eyes to seek out Jack in rebellion.

"And who might you be?"

I turn to the deep, smooth voice of a tall, athletic looking guy dressed all in black. Tilting my head to the side, I drop my eyes down his body, then back up before giving a polite smile. No doubt my mother would have something to say about my lack of subtlety at checking him out.

I take another swig of my drink before holding my hand out to shake his, saying, "Sutton, and you are?"

He takes my hand, dropping a kiss on the back instead of shaking it, as he replies, "Teddy. It's nice to meet you, Sutton. Such an unusual name."

"I'm not so sure about that."

Teddy shifts on his feet, bringing himself half a step closer as a waiter passes by with a tray of mini quiche. "Well, a unique name for a unique beauty. So, who do you know, Jack or Noah?"

Resisting the urge to roll my eyes at his obvious attempt to flirt with me, I straighten my spine, forcing my lips into a demure smile. "I went to the same college as Jack. How about you?"

Teddy looks out over the room, jutting his chin toward a good-looking guy twice his size who looks like he'd be more comfortable on a football field. "Jack, Noah, and I are business partners. Of course, I'm the brains of the operation." Teddy throws a wink at me, smoothing his hand down his tie.

Of course he is. He's an arrogant ass is what he is.

"Come on, Teddy. Don't lie to Sutton like that. We all know you're the face of the operation and I'm the brains."

Taking a sip of my drink, I widen my eyes a fraction to stop myself from closing them as the sound of Jack's smooth, subtle Southern drawl washes over me. *I'm not sure I can do this.*

Before I know it, Jack's arm bands around my waist and I bite down on my tongue to keep the moan in my mouth at such a simple touch. He pulls me into his side, murmuring into my hair, "It's so good to see you, Sutton." He pulls away, holding me at arm's length and I pray he doesn't notice the blush that's no doubt covering me from head to toe from his attention. "You look so good, you're practically glowin'. I can't wait to hear about what you've been up to. Save me some time later, yeah?"

"Sure," I mumble, knowing full well I'll be gone as soon as he leaves.

He squeezes my arms before giving me a slow, sexy smile and looking to his right. "Hey, Noah. Come here."

Noah walks toward us, clapping Jack on the back. "What's up, man?"

"You've spoken to the key players, right?"

Noah looks around before his eyes come back to Jack, a slight furrow to his strong brow. "Yeah."

"Can you keep Sutton company while I finish up?"

My eyes widen, and I reach for my necklace. Rushing to reassure him, I throw out, "Oh, it's okay. I'm totally fine by myself."

Jack lifts a brow at me before looking back to Noah. There's a silent exchange between them before Noah turns to me, holding his arm out and flashing me with a sinful smirk. "Let's get you a refill."

Crap.

And just like that, my plan has gone out the window. *How am I supposed to leave when I've got my own personal babysitter?*

Silver linings, Sutton.

I guess it won't be the end of the world, spending my evening with Noah. He's cute. Okay, maybe cute isn't the right word. He's really hot. Not my normal type, but with the way his physique fills out his suit, he makes me feel small. And right now, his silent and broody vibe matches my mood.

Taking hold of his thick bicep, I allow him to guide me over to the bar.

We spend the rest of the evening talking and getting to know each other. For a moment, disappointment settled in the pit of my stomach that Jack didn't make an effort to circle back to me. Thanks to Noah, it was short-lived.

It's hard to be upset when I leave with my head held high—just like I promised Minnie I would—and the number of a guy who couldn't take his eyes off of me all night.

And as the song goes, if you can't be with the one you love, love the one you're with.

ONE

Jack

I'm sitting in a diner, my eyes trained on the office building door across the road when they should be on the paperwork in front of me. *Christ, I shouldn't even be here.* Six months ago, I was sitting in this very chair, working on my latest project, when my gaze drifted out of the window. I was certain what I was seeing was a figment of my imagination.

What are the chances of me choosing to work in a diner across the road from *her* office? Well, it wasn't my mind playing tricks on me. Fate brought me to this diner, and for months I've been coming back, hoping to have the courage to approach her and ask her to dinner.

Instead, I've watched her leave her building, climb into a town car and drive away. I feel like a fucking addict, desperate for my next fix.

I don't know what the hell is wrong with me.

Despite my rational side telling me this is ridiculous,

I can't stop myself from coming and watching her from the booth by the window. Every time I tell myself this will be the last time, I find myself back here again.

Movement in my peripheral has my gaze darting to the door of her building. Her chestnut brown hair shines in the sun as strands blow around her face in the light breeze. My eyes roam greedily over her as she walks out onto the pavement. It's quiet for the time of day, so I have an unobstructed view of her.

Time seems to stop. Sounds are muted, and it's like we're the only two people in the entire city. Even the chatter of the diner doesn't penetrate my senses. I lean back in the booth as a calm settles over me and I pull in a deep breath.

At least until my attention goes to who she's with. This is the first time she's left with someone. Sutton's talking to a guy, her head thrown back as she laughs heartily. A million questions run through my mind. *Who is he? Why is she laughing? Does she want him?*

My focus goes to where her hand rests on his arm, willing her to move it.

Come on, baby.

I watch as her fingers flex on his bicep, and a fire burns bright inside of me. I'm standing, stuffing my laptop and notebook into my bag. Anger and frustration eat away at my sanity. I refuse to miss my chance again, especially after the fuck up at the investor party for Home 2.0.

My feet move toward the exit of the diner without a

plan. It's not until the sound of the city hits me as I step out onto the sidewalk that I take a moment to calm my frustrated thoughts.

Storming up to her isn't going to achieve anything, except maybe scare her away. No, I need a plan before I even think about approaching her. It's been over a year since we last hung out without a buffer. Christ, I fled the country because I couldn't be around her, as she happily lived her life with my best friend.

I need to be smart about this.

At thirty-two years of age, I can't keep waiting around on the sidelines. Savannah and Noah have taught me that. I either need to move on with my life or make a move.

Pulling on my baseball cap, I keep my head down as I walk in the opposite direction. Away from her. Despite knowing I'm doing the right thing, I can't help but feel a sense of loss as the distance grows.

In a bubble, I don't pay much attention to my surroundings as I walk around the city. My mind is going through a list of pros and cons to acting on the feelings I've tried to bury for years.

Pro: I'd get the girl of my dreams.

Con: She's my best friend's ex, and that goes against bro code.

Pro: I've had feelings for her for thirteen years.

Con: She's shown zero interest in me and I'd likely fuck up our friendship.

No matter what, I keep coming back to that same point.

I. Fucked. Up.

That night four years ago, I should have made an effort to spend time with her. Instead, I let time get away from me, putting business before Sutton. It was a mistake to invite her to that party, but I was so sure I'd be able to carve out some time for her. Never in my wildest dreams did I think she'd end up dating my best friend.

What a fool I was.

I should have invited her to dinner—just the two of us—so I could give her the time and attention she deserves.

Shoulda, woulda, coulda.

I come to a stop outside one of my favorite bakeries. Sweets make everything better. I mean, it won't get me the girl, but I'll feel better with a banana pudding. It's not as good as Mama's, but it scratches the itch.

Pushing through the door, the sweet smell of cakes mixed with the earthy scent of coffee hits me. Grabbing a banana pudding from the fridge by the counter, I hand it over to the cashier before I pick up a spoon from the pot next to the register and open up the creamy goodness.

Walking out, the sun beats down, melting the pudding to the perfect consistency. I gaze up at the concrete jungle surrounding me. New York has a way of making you feel isolated and alone, despite the number of people surrounding you.

It's been a year since I returned to the city and how

have I spent my time? Watching a woman who should be off limits and eating too many cups of banana pudding.

Fuck my life. I'm eating my feelings.

Maybe I need to make some new friends or get a hobby because I can't keep doing this. Burying my feelings in banana pudding isn't going to change my circumstances.

It was a mistake to come back from London.

The thought pops into my head unchecked as a weight settles on my chest. *Should I have stayed away? Would that have been the right thing to do?* I took the coward's way out going to London the first time, but it was what *I* needed.

The idea to go back forms before I can stop it. There are things that I can work on in the lab. And even if there aren't, it's got to be a better path than the one I'm traveling down now.

With my mind made up, I put the lid back on the pudding and throw it in the trash can. *I don't need any more of that tempting goodness.* My strides are purposeful, and since I'm not far from home, I opt to walk. As my feet eat up the sidewalk, I scroll through my phone making arrangements to leave the city, silencing the voice in my head that's calling me out for being a coward.

Again.

TWO

Sutton

I think I might be losing the plot.

Scratch that, I'm certain I already have because for the past six months, it's felt like someone has been watching me. Whenever I leave work, my skin prickles with awareness. It's the strangest feeling because once I'm locked in the safety of the town car, it dissipates.

Each time I leave, I look around, but I haven't seen any faces I recognize. *Would I even see anyone?* The city is huge and there are always crowds everywhere, so maybe whoever it is has kept out of sight.

I'm meeting Ben, Meghan, Savannah, and Alex for lunch today, and I plan on getting their advice. Although, I think I already know what they'll say. No doubt they'll tell me to go to the police and that I should get a body-guard or something equally dramatic.

Maybe it's not a bad idea.

I met Ben, Meghan, and Alex through Savannah. She's Jack's sister and lived with me and Noah for a few months before we split up last year. She's now one of my closest friends, despite the fact that she's now dating my ex.

Thankfully, it's not awkward between us. Savannah and Noah are much better suited than he and I ever were. Our first couple of years together were really good, but after a point—I'm not sure when—I think we only stayed together because we made sense on paper. The truth is, our feelings were never all-consuming, but we were comfortable with each other and so I think we settled.

I'm the last to arrive at the restaurant today, although that's nothing new lately. I've been filling my time with work to the point of exhaustion. I guess that's what happens when you don't have anybody to go home to. Although, on a more positive note, my business has grown beyond my wildest dreams and I'm taking on more and more international clients.

On Monday, I fly out to London to meet with a Lord planning a sixtieth birthday bash for his wife. I travel back to New York on Wednesday to meet with a Saudi prince before flying out to Vegas to meet with a hotel heiress on Friday.

Following the maitre'd through the restaurant, I adjust the belt on my wide leg linen trousers, suddenly nervous to share my suspicions. I know they'll take me seriously, but I feel like speaking about it is going to make it so much more real.

For the first time in my life, I feel unsafe. Growing up with a politician for a father, there were times when threats were made, but I was wrapped securely in my bubble, and for the most part, oblivious to the dangers.

When we arrive at the table, I'm pulled into hugs before I can even say hello. The server waits patiently at the side to take my drink order, and I'm bombarded with what feels like a million questions asking how I'm doing, how I got my hair to curl like it is, where I got my shirt from... It goes some way to easing the tension I've felt building inside of me all day.

I order two dirty martinis—a little Dutch courage to get the words out. When the chatter dies down as we study the menus, I lean back in my chair, trying to focus on the words in front of me. I told myself I'd wait until we'd ordered to broach the subject, but I can't wait. It's like a weight resting on my chest, desperate to be lifted.

Closing the menu, I lay it down on the table before pulling in a deep breath and blurting, "I think someone's following me."

God, I sound neurotic.

Ben looks up and around the restaurant, his brow furrowed. "Like right now?"

Shaking my head, I reply, "No. So, maybe following isn't the right word. For the past six months, when I finish work and I'm leaving my building, it feels like somebody's watching me. I've thought about calling the police, but I don't have any evidence other than a feeling. Which isn't anything to act on."

Putting her menu down, Alex rests her elbows on the table as she speaks. "You should call the police. I hate to be that person, but this is how women are murdered, Sutton. Definitely take this seriously. We can come with you if you like."

My attention goes to Savannah. Her eyes are slightly narrowed as she stares at Alex before smoothing her brow out. *That's odd.* "Hold on. If she has no evidence, surely they won't be able to do anythin'?"

Meghan takes a sip of her drink as she shrugs, "It's better to have the report logged than to not, God forbid anything did happen. I would go to the police, file the report, and maybe look at getting some security."

I know this is serious and that this could go badly, but I still find myself trying to downplay the situation. "Honestly, I don't know that anything would happen. It just feels like someone is watching me. It's not like I have a crazy ex or deal with creepy customers on a daily basis. I think if someone wanted to do something, they'd have done it by now, right?"

My question hangs in the air before Ben leans across the table, taking hold of my hand. He gives it a gentle squeeze as he asks, "Did you feel like you were being followed here?"

"No. Like I said, it's only when I'm leaving the office. Maybe it's all in my imagination?" It comes out as a question. Desperation coats my words as I look around the table at my friends' sympathetic faces.

Ben pulls back his hand, his voice is soothing when he says, "That's good. Have you been receiving any messages, things left in your mailbox, or random deliveries being made?"

"No."

"And you don't have the same feeling when you're at home?"

"Thankfully, no."

Ben smiles reassuringly. "This is really good. It doesn't look like they've gone beyond watching you at work, but it doesn't mean they won't. I agree with the girls. You should report it."

Alex picks up her drink, taking a sip before asking, "And you really have no clue who it could be? There's nobody that you've blown off recently or a client that was a bit too 'friendly'?"

"No. None of my clients would have the time to stalk me. I haven't dated anyone since Noah and I broke up, and I definitely haven't turned anyone down."

Savannah picks up her menu, keeping her eyes focused on it as she asks, "Why do you feel that you're being watched? If you haven't seen anyone or received anything creepy, what, besides a feeling, makes you think someone is watching you?"

My brows tug together as I reply, "It's just a creepy feeling. My skin prickles and my heart races. I don't know how else to describe it." I offer up a smile that feels like a lie as I say, "I've told you guys, but if I'm still feeling this way by the end of the week, I'll go to the police."

With a sympathetic smile, Meghan says, "If you're sure. Like Alex said, we'll come with you."

I'm not sure at all.

"I'm sure. Enough about me. What has everyone been up to? I feel like it's been weeks since we last caught up."

Alex eyes me suspiciously, as if she doesn't quite believe me, while Ben is back to looking around the restaurant for my 'stalker'. Savannah is engrossed in the menu, which is surprising since she knows it by heart, seeing as this is our usual brunch spot.

Meghan has a soft smile on her face that tells me she's going to provide me with the perfect distraction before she even opens her mouth. "Well, I've been trying to keep up with a two-year-old and a one-year-old that are conspiring against me. It's as if they have a plan of attack drawn up each day that they put into action as soon as Cooper steps out the door."

Meghan and Cooper, her husband, met at work. Cooper is a lawyer and Meghan was his assistant. I don't know all the details, but in a nutshell, they had a thing and now they have two of the most adorable toddlers I've ever met.

Ben offers, "Well, you know you can call me anytime to come and spend time with them. I've been remodeling the house as a little side project, working at the hospital and probably clubbing a little too much. I could do with some wholesome toddler company."

He lives on the same street as Meghan; it's how they met and he recently broke up with a guy he was seeing. I think he was more heartbroken than he let on.

Meghan laughs, a cheeky glint in her eyes when she responds. "If you want to take my cute little demons off of my hands one afternoon, please feel free. I swear, it's like Cooper doesn't believe me because they are as sweet as pie when he steps back through the door."

Alex holds her hands up, leaning back in her chair. "Don't even look at me for childcare. I'm too busy practicing with my husband to even consider having babies at the minute."

Leaning forward, Meghan pins Alex with her gaze. "But you're going to, right? I need to not be the only mom in this friendship group."

At the desperate plea in her tone, we erupt into loud laughter, drawing attention from the other diners around us. This was just what I needed to ease some of the concern that was threatening to consume me.

THREE

Jack

My door bangs against the wall as Savannah bursts through, making me jump in my spot on the couch. *Great, I'll probably have to get that replastered.* She looks a little wild and a whole lot crazy as she storms across the living room to stand in front of me. My sister has a flair for the dramatic. I shouldn't be surprised, given the fact that she's an actress.

Why did I give her the passcode for the door?

I pause the TV, turning my attention to her, knowing full well that she won't leave until she's told me whatever it is that has her so worked up.

Her usually sweet southern accent is harsh and accusing, something I haven't heard since we were kids. "I swear to all that is holy, if you been stalkin' Sutton, I'll skin you like a coon that's ripped through the attic, Jack O'Riley."

Oh shit.

How do I even answer that? Honestly?

If only it was that fucking easy. I guess technically I haven't been stalking Sutton, but how do I justify watching her from across the street of her office building? The simple answer is, I can't. What I've been doing is wrong, and even though I know that, I can't seem to stop. It's why I'm leaving.

I must take too long to answer as Savannah reaches out and smacks me across the back of my head. She drops onto the sofa next to me, open slaps raining down on me as she mutters like a mad woman.

At my lack of reaction—let's face it, her hands are tiny and barely hurt—she turns away, huffing back into the couch cushions. Smoothing a hand over her forehead, she sighs, "I can't believe you, Jack."

Unable to take the disappointment wrapping around her, I hold up my hands; the lie falling from my lips before I can stop it. "Hey, I didn't do anything."

She leans back, facing me with a brow raised in question. "Really?"

My body sags with defeat under her scrutiny. *Fuck, why can't I keep anything from her?* "Fine, I may or may not have been watching Sutton. But that's all it was."

As if that makes it any better.

"What the hell, Jack? She's going to call the police because she's freaked out!"

Blowing out a breath, I run my fingers through my hair. "I didn't mean to scare her. I just... I can't seem to stay away. She consumes me, and yet she wants nothing to do with me. I don't know what to do, Sav, but I know I can't stay in the city."

"First of all, have you even asked her if she wants nothing to do with you? And second of all, again? 'Cause that worked out so well for you last time." Savannah folds her arms, staring at me pointedly.

Frustration takes root in the pit of my stomach, and I stand from the couch, pacing in front of her. I ignore her first question. Too much rides on me voicing it, but I know Sutton is much too good for me. We come from different backgrounds. For one, I grew up in a house that lived paycheck to paycheck, where she met presidents and royalty. What could she ever see in a guy like me?

My voice is loud as I bellow, "Do you think I haven't tried to get over her? Why the hell do you think I left for London in the first place, Sav, because it sure wasn't for work? I've been infatuated with Sutton since college, and I couldn't stand watching her as she fell deeper and deeper in *love* with my best friend." I pull in a breath before continuing, "And now you tell me that I've been scaring her? Tell me how leaving isn't the right thing to do when I can't stop myself from seeking her out? When she's afraid of my behavior?"

As if she hasn't heard a word I've said, Savannah replies, her voice an octave too cheery, "Okay, I'll help you."

My brow furrows, disbelief bubbling out of me in a

puff. Turning to face her, I ask, "Did you not hear a word I just said?"

"Of course. And what I got from it is you don't know *how* to get the girl. Well, big brother, I'm gonna help you do just that. You shoulda come to me months ago, but it's okay. The main thing is that you've come to me now."

"What do you mean, I should have come to you months ago?" My brow furrows as my heart beats an unsteady rhythm.

Savannah at least has the sense to look away sheepishly. She jumps over the back of the couch as if it will offer her some sort of protection. There's a touch of hesitation in her voice when she says, "Well, it's just, you haven't exactly been subtle about how much you like her. I've been waiting for you to ask me for help. I didn't want to force the issue but I had an inkling you were interested when you walked in on me and Noah last year. Okay, more than an inkling, because it was like a giant neon sign that you were more concerned about her than me. It took me a while after, looking back at the conversation, to figure it out."

I thought I was at least being covert about it.

A weight settles in my stomach and my palms become clammy. "Does Noah know?"

Savannah tilts her head to the side, a sympathetic smile on her mouth. "Of course he does, Jack. Not subtle, remember?"

Fuck.

Turning away, I dive my fingers into my hair, pulling

on the strands as my mind races with solutions to the problem. There's only one.

"Well, that's settled then... I'm leaving the city."

I turn in the direction of my bedroom, coming up short when Savannah appears in front of me. She stretches, resting her hands on my shoulders as she forces me to maintain eye contact.

"You're not going anywhere, unless it's to go and declare your feelings for Sutton. Noah doesn't care, Jack. He just wants you to be happy... and stay in the city."

I take a step back as her words sink in. I must be dreaming. In what universe does my best friend not have any feelings about me dating his ex? *Probably the same one in which I don't have many feelings about him dating my sister.* Still, I've been using his possible objection as a reason to not make a move on Sutton. Without that, there's really only one reason to hold back and how strong of a reason is that?

Oblivious to my inner turmoil, Savannah takes a seat, chattering about her grand plan and how I should've just come to her in the first place.

I cut her off, certainty coating my words. "I can't stay, Sav. Even if I wanted to, you said yourself that she's scared. I don't want to be someone she's afraid of."

With a firm grip, Savannah guides me to the couch, pushing me back onto the black cushions. She drops to her knees in front of me, forcing me to look at her. In a tone I'd expect someone to use with a child, she says, "She's only afraid because of the uncertainty. Anyone would be, not knowing who's out there watching you. Have you told her how you feel?"

I know what she's going to say when I tell her no, but she doesn't understand how it's not as simple as telling Sutton I have feelings for her. A lot rides on this. The last thing I want to do is lose any semblance of her friendship that I still have, and if she's uncomfortable with me wanting more, that's exactly what's going to happen.

"I'm going to take your silence as a no. Did you know that nine years ago at the house party you and Noah crashed, that I made a pass at him?"

My brows shoot to my hairline. I'm torn between wanting to know why she's telling me that, needing to know what happened, and tracking my friend down to find out why *he* didn't tell me.

"Calm down, Jack. I'm telling you because I put myself out there for him and he shut me down. It hurt like hell but I got over it. If you don't try, you'll never know."

But they also didn't see each other for years after. She might think I didn't notice, but it was pretty obvious when he'd be around that she'd make up an excuse to leave.

Even taking that into account, I can't dismiss the fact that they're together now, and as much as I hate it, she has a point. I just can't get rid of the nagging sensation in my gut. If I put myself out there with Sutton, I risk losing a genuine friendship, and those are hard to come by.

"You do realize you'll lose her either way if you run

away? I can't believe for one second that you'd rather have a ghost of a friendship than tell her how you feel. That's not the big brother I know."

Great, now she's guilt tripping me into making a fool of myself *and* reading my mind. *But she has a point. Again.* "If—and it's a big if, Sav—I was to let you help me, what would the plan look like?"

Savannah bursts up doing her ridiculous happy dance before collapsing onto the couch next to me. Excitedly, she runs through a plan on how I can 'woo'—as she puts it—Sutton.

By the time she's done, I've got to admit, if Sutton has any feelings for me that aren't purely platonic, it might just work.

FOUR

Sutton

I'm putting the last of my toiletries into my suitcase when there's a knock at my apartment door. My hands pause mid air, shampoo in one and conditioner in the other. A shiver races down my spine as I straighten and tentatively move through my apartment. I know it won't be any of my friends 'just dropping by'. They know I'm going out of town and usually send a text before turning up out of the blue.

What if it's whoever's been watching me?

As I step over the threshold and into the living room, my heart races. My phone sits on charge on the little table next to the couch. Shaking out my trembling hands, I race across the room and swipe it up and move, as quietly as possible, toward the front door. The whole time, I pray whoever is on the other side has gone.

One at a time, I rest my hands on the back of the door,

leaning in. The sound of my breathing is magnified in the quiet of the apartment. My eye isn't quite at the peephole when they knock again. Smacking my hand over my mouth to keep myself from letting out a yelp of surprise, my eyes widen a touch as I will my racing heart to slow down.

Jesus, Sutton, it's probably a delivery person.

Closing one eye, I look through the peephole. It's like a weight being lifted. My shoulders drop as my body sags against the wood.

It's Jack.

It feels like forever since I've seen him. I guess that's what happens when someone is such a fixture in your life and then one day they just disappear with barely a goodbye.

I frown. He's never been here, so I'm not sure how he knows where I live. Still, a different kind of nervousness attacks me as I get my fill and take him in through the peephole. This one causes a fluttering in my stomach and a weakness in my knees.

This one is wholly inappropriate.

He's supposed to *only* be my friend. But I can't help that the feelings I had for him in college returned the first time I saw him after my breakup with Noah. Like they were still bubbling beneath the surface and threatening to erupt at the mere sight of him.

Get it together, Sutton.

Sucking in a breath, I smooth one hand over my black yoga pants as I pull open the door with the other. A smile forms on my lips as I say, "Hey Jack. It's been a while. Is everything okay?"

His voice is like Tennessee whiskey—or Alabama, since that's where he's from—smooth and yet raspy at the same time. There's an uncertainty about him when he replies, "Hi Sutton. Have you got a minute?"

It's not like Jack to skip the niceties. *Is something wrong with Savannah?* I step back from the door, signaling for him to enter. When he crosses the threshold, he thrusts a bunch of tulips into my arms and I blink at them in confusion.

He looks on edge as his gaze roams around the room before landing back on me. "It's a nice place ya got here. Did you move in long ago?"

What the hell is going on?

A mix of curiosity and uncertainty that I can't hide fills my tone as I reply, "Thank you. I moved in after Noah and I split."

He looks away, his jaw ticking before he blows out a breath. His gaze drops to the floor and then he lifts his blue eyes and says, "Of course."

Neither of us speaks for a moment. The sound of the city twenty floors below us is barely audible and yet with the silence between us, it's all I can hear.

Jack scrubs a hand over the back of his neck before continuing, "I was wondering if you'd like to go out for dinner with me."

A smile forms on my lips, and I release a relieved breath that nothing is wrong. Why is he nervous about going to dinner? "Of course. It would be great to catch up."

He stuffs his hands into the pockets of his black jeans, his shoulders lifting to his ears. "As a date, Sutton."

Oh. Not at all what I expected him to say.

My fingers search for the gold necklace around my neck, fiddling with the delicate chain. I don't know what to say. How do I respond to that? My immediate response is to say yes, but he's never shown me an ounce of interest before, so why now?

Turning away and leaving his question unanswered, I force myself to walk into the kitchen, digging through the cabinets for a vase. Anything to occupy myself. Jack follows, leaning against the doorjamb, content to wait for my response as he watches me fill the vase with water and start preparing the stems.

When I can no longer take the silence, I turn to face him, a tulip in one hand and the kitchen scissors in the other. "Why? Why do you want to go on a date?"

He pushes away from the frame, taking a step toward me. I take one back, my behind hitting the counter. Jack stops, running his fingers through the slightly long strands of his hair. "Why not?"

Why not? Is he being serious right now? I can list at least a million reasons why not. One, he's never shown any interest in me before. Two, I'm likely to fall in love with him—if I'm not already. Three, he'll break my heart. Not intentionally, but he will.

As much as I want to say yes, to ask him what's taken

him so long. I know that our time has passed and any chance we had of being together is long gone.

It's just one date.

Turning back to the counter, I ignore the voice in my head.

"It doesn't have to mean anything if you don't want it to, Sutton."

Closing my eyes, I put the scissors and flower down as my chin drops to my chest and the first crack appears in my heart. That's the problem. I'd want it to mean so much more than I think he realizes. It's why I have to force out my next words. Facing Jack, I lift my chin and lie, "I have no interest in going on a date with you, Jack. Please, can we just leave it at that?"

For some reason, I expect him to put up a fight, and for a moment, as he stares at me from across the room, I think he just might. In fact, I want him to fight for me, to tell me that he wants me just the way I am.

I see the moment he decides against it. My stomach clenches and heaviness settles over me.

Please leave.

"*Fuck.*" He turns away from me before coming to a stop. "I'm sorry I put this on you. If you do ever want to grab dinner, as friends, you know where I am."

Jack doesn't wait for me to respond and when the soft click of the front door confirms he's left, I release my death grip on the counter.

Have I just made the biggest mistake of my life?

No, we missed our time.

I shake out my hands as nausea hits me like a tidal wave. Pushing away the thoughts and burying the feelings—like I was raised to do—I arrange the flowers he brought me before returning to my bedroom to finish packing.

It's been over a year and a half since Noah and I split up. I haven't even considered dating since although it's not like I haven't been asked. Maybe I should put myself back out there. Get back on the horse, as Minnie would say.

With the vase of tulips in one arm, I swipe up my phone as I walk back to my bedroom. My fingers dart across the screen as I scroll through my call log for Minnie's name. She's the perfect person to ask for help when it comes to dating. She keeps a log of the most eligible and desirable men in the city. Bringing the phone to my ear, I wait for the call to connect.

"Darling Sutton, I miss you, lovely lady."

Minnie is what most would call a socialite. She has a tendency to defy anyone who tells her what to do, hence why she's currently abroad. Her father told her she needed to 'focus and learn what the real world's like if she wants to have a cent more from him' and so she thought she'd rebel and spend a fortune on a vacation.

We're polar opposites, but with our similar upbringings, we bonded the moment we met twenty years ago. Minnie is my person, even when she's jet-setting around the world.

Some of the tension eases from my shoulders and I

chuckle down the line. "I miss you too. What country are you in today?"

"Oh, you know, one that's hot and with plenty of virile men."

"I wouldn't expect anything else. When are you back in the city?"

"I have two more weeks of bliss before I have to come back to reality. One second, darling." Muffled chatter and laughter sound on the other end of the call before the background noise comes back to full clarity. "Sorry about that, something... came up. Let me go somewhere with some privacy and then you can tell me what's happened."

It's just like Minnie to know when I need her. When she's settled, I explain the Jack situation before pulling in a deep breath and blurting out, "I need you to set me up with someone. It's time I got back out there."

Hesitation coats her words. "Are you sure? Last I checked, you were still over the moon for that man. Don't you think you should explore that before shutting down that possibility?"

"I'm sure. Just because he finally asked me out doesn't mean he wants a relationship. You should have heard him. He may as well have been ordering takeout. It wouldn't mean the same thing to him as it does to me, and then where does that leave me? I'll be more hopelessly in love with him than I already am."

"Darling, I hate to break it to you, but that's the whole point of dating. You fall in love with him, he falls in love with you. Poof. Happily ever after. And this whole having nothing to offer thing is total bullshit. He was on the cover of *Forbes*, darling, he doesn't need anything *from* you. He just needs *you*."

That's the problem and it always will be. I wish, more than anything, that what Minnie was saying was true, but Jack deserves a woman who has *something* to offer him. He deserves someone that challenges him and drives him to be the best man he can, while bringing more than her connections—from her parents—to the table. Connections he doesn't even need.

With a determination that doesn't quite seem real, I reply, "I'm thirty-one, Minnie. I've got to move on from a crush that started when I was eighteen."

Minnie is quiet for so long that I have to pull the phone away from my ear to check we're still connected. "Why don't we go for dinner when I get back? If you're still feeling the same way, I'll go through my matchmaker questions and get to work finding you a man?"

I collapse onto the bed, resting my hand on my collarbone. "Yes, that sounds perfect. Thank you, Minnie."

We spend the next twenty minutes on the phone as Minnie updates me on her escapades. When we end the call, I've managed to convince myself that turning Jack down was the right thing to do. I can't keep pining over a man I can't have.

FIVE

Jack

This has got to be the craziest thing I've ever done.

Am I really chartering a private jet to take me from New York to London so I can plead my case to the woman who turned me down a matter of days ago? I should've had them drop me off at a hospital because this is not what 'normal'—whatever that looks like—people do.

Having my sister find out where she's staying definitely doesn't help my case. Should I be restrained in a straight jacket? Possibly. I don't know why I thought this crazy plan was a good idea. Okay, so it wasn't exactly my idea, but I'm the older sibling and when Savannah suggested it, I should've said no.

I'm definitely questioning my sanity as I follow Sutton down the bustling London sidewalk, my cap low over my brow. She walks into a coffee shop; the door closing behind her and shutting off my access. I cross the street and come to a stop in front of a store window.

What am I even doing?

Technically, this is stalking and regardless of the country I'm in, it's illegal. This is a step above the watching her from a diner in New York. I know it's wrong and yet I'm not leaving. My feet are still rooted to the spot, my focus on the door she walked through, rather than the display in front of me.

Shoving my hands into my jeans pockets, I hunch my shoulders while my eyes are trained on the reflection of the coffee shop in the glass. I'm oblivious to my surroundings, on a mission to find the perfect time to approach her.

"What do you think you're doing?"

Shit. I guess now is that time.

The accusation is thrown out furiously from a woman I know all too well. Turning to face Sutton, I pull my cap off and run my fingers through my hair. A blush creeps over my cheeks at being caught. Injecting as much innocence into my tone as possible, I reply, "Oh hey, Sutton. Fancy seeing you here."

"Jack, what the hell do you think you're doing?"

"Just browsing." The words trail off as I look over my shoulder and into the window of the store I was using as my personal rearview mirror. A big white cloud of fabric adorning a mannequin glows back at me.

As if the store I'm using as my cover is a bridal boutique.

Cocking a brow, Sutton juts her hip as she puts a

hand on the other. "Really? Because it looks like you were following me."

Holding my hands up, I take a step back as I say, "Okay, I get that it looks like that..."

There's a furious fire burning bright in her eyes. Her voice is raised and nothing like the Sutton she shows the world. It stirs something to life in my gut as she spits, "It is like that, Jack. This is unbelievable. Is this because I turned you down for a date? Did you think you'd try some light stalking to get me to say yes?"

Sutton sucks in a breath and I watch, fascinated, as the shutters come down, her spine straightens and *Debutante Sutton* comes out. I hate that she can't allow herself to express her annoyance, that she feels like she has to put on a show even with me.

Closing her eyes, she squeezes the bridge of her nose before opening them on an exhale and asking, "Don't you see how crazy this is?"

I blow out an exasperated breath, dropping my chin to my chest, before looking her in the eye and saying, "Of course I do, but—"

She shakes her head, cutting me off as she lifts her chin and states, "There are no buts, Jack. You've *followed* me to London. That's extreme, even for you."

My words tumble from my lips before I can stop them, self-preservation kicking in. "I have work here. It's a coincidence, nothing more."

Sutton eyes me skeptically. She has every right to. I'm lying. There is no work. I want her, and it's on the tip of my tongue to come clean and tell her that I've wanted her to be mine since the day we met. That I'll do anything to have her, to make her feel seen and cherished like she deserves to be.

So why isn't she mine?

Because I'm a fucking coward and she's too good for me.

It's like a light going off in her mind as she connects the dots. "Have you been watching me outside my office?" When I don't respond, she continues, "Don't even *think* about lying to me, Jack O'Riley."

A shot of desire rips through me at the sound of my name on her lips. The crowd bustles around us and I take a step forward, causing Sutton to tilt her chin and look me in the eye. I need to distract her from the depths of my obsession because if she finds out, she'll run as far away from me as she possibly can and I'll have ruined my shot.

"Give me *one* date."

One date to show her how good we'd be together. To prove to her that I'm all in. That I see her for who she really is. Although, I'll have to be subtle about it because I don't want to scare her off, not when she's way out of my league.

She drops her gaze from mine and shakes her head as she looks down the street. "I don't know, Jack."

It feels like she's holding herself back, and I'm not sure what's stopping her from saying yes. Does she only want something casual? Sav did say she hadn't dated anyone in a while. Maybe that's the issue. She thinks I'm after something serious—which I am—but she doesn't want that.

Gently, I move her chin so she's forced to look at me. The sounds of the city are muted as I look into the depths of her dark brown eyes. "One date and I'll walk away."

Little does she know, there's not a fucking chance of that happening.

But if it's what I've got to tell her to get her to go to dinner with me, then I'll tell this little white lie. Sutton's gaze searches mine, for what, I'm not sure. But I pray to God that she doesn't see my truth. That she agrees to this one date.

Uncertainty weighs down her words when she repeats, "I don't know." Her tongue darts out to lick her lips and I don't miss the way her focus drops to my own. Distracted, she asks, "It'll just be one date, right?"

I don't fight the urge to swipe my thumb over her full bottom lip as I take a step closer. Our chests brush and her audible gasp at our proximity is like music to my ears. I know in this moment that when we happen, we'll be explosive. "Yeah, it'll just be one date," I assure her.

It's barely audible, but I don't miss it when she breathes out, "Okay."

I want to jump for joy. To climb up Big Ben and tell the whole of London that my *dream woman* is going to go out with me. It's like I've won the fucking lottery.

Instead, I pull down a mask, taking a step back from her. The loss of her warmth leaves me feeling robbed, but I nod, feigning nonchalance. "I'll pick you up at seven."

Her lips are parted, and her eyes are wide as she looks at me. Sutton nods and I watch the movement of her throat as she swallows before I leave.

Walking away is hard, but with my back to her, I allow a giant grin to spread across my face. I have plans to put in motion, because if this is my one chance, I'm damn well not gonna fuck it up.

Tonight *has* to be perfect.

SIX

Sutton

W hy didn't I agree to go on this date sooner? So far it's the best date I've ever been on, which is saying something considering we've just been shown to our table.

Jack's been a true gentleman, opening doors for me, making sure I'm walking on the building side of the sidewalk, and offering me his jacket because I apparently forgot I wasn't in the midst of a New York summer.

But I can already tell this is only going to end one way; with *my* heart being broken.

The thought has me sitting up straighter in my seat as I place the white linen napkin across my lap. My hand shakes when I lift the menu to read through it. I'm not hungry. Nerves have taken over my stomach, and I'm not sure I could manage a bite. My whole body feels so tense it might shatter.

I can feel Jack's eyes on me, even as my own try to

make out the words on the page. *Why does he have to look so good tonight?* When he picked me up at the hotel, it took every ounce of self control to not grab hold of his tie and drag him to my room.

As hard as I try to stop them, my eyes move to the hand he rests on the table as he leans forward. *Do they have to be so wide and lean with those sexy popping veins?*

His voice is low, as if he's trying to protect me from anyone else hearing him call me out. "You can relax, you know."

Exhaling on a laugh, I peer up at him from under my lashes. Honesty should always be the best policy, at least that's what my grandma drilled into me since I was little. I swallow thickly before lifting my chin and looking anywhere but at Jack. The words tumbling from my mouth are not entirely untrue. "I'm nervous."

I'm also confused as to why I'm even here. What are his motives for asking me out? It's not *really* a date, is it? The questions fight to be asked as my heart pounds in my chest.

The longer we stare at each other, the more the air crackles between us. Unable to take a second more, I rip my gaze away and shift in my seat. I shouldn't be turned on by him, not when he's been nothing but friendly to me. *It's all in my imagination.* There's no way Jack wants me like *that*. Yes, he asked me on a date, but it doesn't mean anything in the grand scheme of things.

When Jack doesn't speak, I glance over to find him leaning back in his chair, an easy smile on his lips. Self conscious, my hand lifts to my face before going to my hair as I ask, "What?"

He raises a brow, the smile transforming into a smug grin. "Why the hell are you nervous around me? We've known each other for years, Sutton. Take a breath and get rid of the pressure you're putting on yourself. Don't make it more than this moment."

Right, basically stop worrying because this is just two friends having dinner. Nothing more, nothing less.

Jack is... God, I don't know what he's feeling or even thinking, but I'm over here freaking out. Those crazy big feelings from years ago are on the precipice of spiraling dangerously out of control at the smallest sign of encouragement from him. I can practically feel them hovering above me, haunting me. It's only a matter of time before they drop, coating me in unrequited love, yet again. Sucking in a breath, I hold it for a second before exhaling and forcing myself to relax.

I'm overreacting, that's all.

Straightening my spine, I apologize, "Forgive me. It's been a while since I last went out with a guy. I think I just got into my head. How is work going?" I pick up the menu, pretending to browse the mains as I wait for Jack to answer. In truth, the words are a jumble in front of me, and I want nothing more than to tell him this was a mistake and leave.

Why does it feel so awkward?

How can it feel like a blind date when we've known each

other for thirteen years? That's it. I'm not going to let my feelings ruin this evening.

His voice is gravelly, with a gruffness to it that I've never heard from him before. It's almost like he's mad, but that can't be right. What would he have to be mad about? "You really want to talk about work?"

"What else do you talk about when you go out for dinner?"

Jack's laughter rumbling from his chest is probably my new favorite sound, even if it is at my own expense. I've never been more grateful for low lighting and blusher. My cheeks heat before my entire body warms from head to toe. Dropping my head, I allow the grin that spreads over my face at having made him happy to grow bright and wide.

"It's really been a while since you went on a date, huh?"

If only he knew. When Noah and I were together, especially toward the end, any time we went out for dinner, our conversations were filled with work. It's been years since I went on a first date—*not that this is one*—so I'm a little out of practice.

Chancing a look at Jack, I study him. He's not traditionally handsome, yet he's still the most attractive man I've ever laid eyes on. His two front teeth overlap, but only by a fraction. His jaw looks freshly shaved and amusement always lights up his blue eyes.

There's a slight crook to his nose but I've never found out how it happened, I just know that somewhere in the six or so years between college and seeing each other again, he must have broken it.

Dark brown hair, which my fingers are itching to glide through, flops over his forehead. Jack has always reminded me of Dimitri from *Anastasia*. It was one of my favorite films growing up, with him being one of my favorite characters. I guess it makes sense that I'd find Jack attractive.

"Anyway." I lift my chin, correct my posture, and pull my thoughts back to the moment. "This isn't a date, so what does it matter what we talk about?"

Jack puts down his menu, his hand resting on the table. I drag my eyes away from the veins, only to get lost in the depths of his blue gaze. There's a seriousness to his tone that doesn't quite match the lightness in his eyes when he asks, "What would you call it then?"

Taking a sip of my water, I set the glass down and fold my hands into my lap. With as much certainty as I can inject into my tone, I reply, "This is just dinner between two friends."

Jack presses his lips together into a fine line, his brows raising before he looks away. Fascinated, I watch the ticking muscle in his jaw and momentarily, I'm distracted. An urge to climb across the table and lick the thick column of his neck floors me.

Where did that come from?

Yes, I'm attracted to him and have been for a long time, but never have I wanted to do anything so... primal. When I get back to New York, I need to sort my life out.

Get a work-life balance. Find a guy to date. Maybe get a puppy. *Anything* to stop these inappropriate thoughts.

Clearing my throat, I drop my eyes to my lap, needing a moment to get myself back in check. Jesus, I just claimed he's nothing more than a friend before having seriously inappropriate thoughts about him.

Coming here was a really bad idea.

"Do you remember what I asked you for earlier today?"

My brows furrow and I lift my focus back to Jack, curious as to what he means. "Do you mean when you asked me to dinner?"

"Yes."

I don't understand what point he's trying to prove, but I'll humor him. "You asked me to go out for dinner?"

Shaking his head, Jack pins me with his stare. "No, Sutton, I asked you for one date. Don't you dare sit there and tell me that this is 'just dinner between two friends'."

Something about the command in his tone that brokers no argument has my insides fluttering. Raising my hand, I rest it on my collar, the racing of my heart pulsing under my palm a reminder of my current reality. My response is no more than a breathless whisper of "Okay."

He stares at me for a moment before nodding his head and returning to study his menu. "Good. Now what're you gonna order?"

I don't have a hope of making out what's on the

menu when I have a single question begging to be voiced. Sitting forward, I rest my elbows on the table—sorry Mom. Jack lifts his head from the menu, tilting it a fraction in question.

"Why?"

Why did you follow me to London? One question at a time.

Jack rests his menu on the table in front of him. He's still leaning back in his chair, his eyes moving around the restaurant before he scrubs a hand over his jaw and lifts a shoulder in a shrug. "I guess I wanted to see if there was anything between us. When we were in college, it felt like there might have been, but neither of us acted on it. You're single, I'm single, so why not?"

Right.

My shoulders sag before I catch myself and snap back up. A heaviness settles in my body, threatening to collapse me over the table. If I could trust my legs, I'd leave, or at least excuse myself to the bathroom. I've been over here worrying about falling in love with him and he's looking at this like it's a casual exploration of whether or not we might click as more than friends.

Quieter than I'd like, I ask, "So that's all this is? Something casual to see if we have a connection?"

That's what I was telling myself moments ago, but to hear him confirm it hurts. I hold my breath, waiting for him to reply.

"Yeah, that's all it is." He shrugs his shoulders.

"If it is, then why did you follow me to London? You could have called me when I got home?"

Jack breaks eye contact with me, looking out over the restaurant before he speaks. "I don't know. It was kind of a spur-of-the-moment thing."

I press my lips together, fiddling with the delicate chain around my neck. Jack has always been a calculated guy. Every move he's made has been thought through and the pros and cons weighed up. This doesn't make sense.

With a heavy sigh, he runs his fingers through his hair as he says, "Let's just enjoy this evening. If we don't have fun, we can chalk it up to two friends having dinner and if we do, then we can talk about what we want."

Studying him for a moment, I think over what he's just said. On the surface, without him knowing the depths of my feelings back when we were in college, what he's suggesting is reasonable. But I know me and how I felt. I don't know how I get out of this unscathed.

I'll sit through dinner, give him his date, and get reacquainted with my *friend*, but Jack and I are on two different pages and I won't put my heart on the line in the hopes he'll want more.

SEVEN

Jack

"**A**nd that is how I saved the day and now have a favor owed to me by the Prime Minister." I sip on my drink, a smug smile on my face.

Sutton laughs, the sound wrapping me in its warmth. Over the course of this evening, it's grown to become my most favorite sound. *Again.*

"I don't believe that for a second."

Heat fills my face and I look down at the plate in front of me. "Fine. Maybe I've exaggerated a little."

She leans forward, the corner of her lips lifting with her brows. "Just a little?"

"Yeah, only a little. He does owe me, though."

A comfortable quiet falls over us. Sutton leans back in her chair, a hand going to her stomach. "What are you going to ask him for?"

My answer is almost instantaneous. "The keys to the Kingdom, of course."

White teeth drag over her bottom lip. "I hate to break it to you, but that isn't likely to happen. You've got to have something else you want?"

You.

Pushing away my plate, I hold her eyes as I say, "The truth is, he doesn't have anything I want."

The air's charged around us and the restaurant might as well be empty for all the attention we're paying to it. I'm painfully aware of each breath I take, focusing on it to keep my body still. She's the one for me and tonight has cemented it.

The cheerful server arrives next to the table, his question cutting through the tension. "Was everything to your satisfaction?"

My voice comes out a rasp. "Yes, thank you."

"Would you like to see the dessert menu?"

I raise a brow at Sutton, but she shakes her head. Dipping my head, I try to hide the disappointment that's no doubt showing on my face. As much as I don't want this night to end, I can't force her to stay here, and even if she did, the restaurant would kick us out eventually.

"Shall we have another drink?" she suggests.

Yes. God, yes.

Tampering down the excitement bubbling away in the pit of my stomach, I reply, "Sure. Let's get another round."

A delicate smile pulls at her lips. Sutton's voice is gentle and there's a hint of reluctance in there when she says, "I'm going to the bathroom."

We stand, staring at each other until she mutters something under her breath and walks to the back of the restaurant. Like a lovesick fool, I watch the gentle sway of her hips as she goes.

I need a plan. At this point, Savannah's idea has gone out the window. Now, I need something to make tonight last longer to get her to see how good together we are. I think she's close, especially as her guards come down as the night has worn on, but nothing in life is guaranteed and it's very likely I could be wrong.

EIGHT

Sutton

Raindrops fall in a heavy curtain from the inky black sky when we leave the restaurant. There's a musicality to the rain as it drums on the floor, the sound of the city fighting to be heard over it. We're huddled under the ease in a bid to stay dry, the heat from his body warming mine in more ways than one.

My mom would be so mad at me right now for not being prepared. I can practically hear her chastising tone as goosebumps break out over my exposed skin. First, I forgot my coat, and now, because I chose fashion over practicality, I don't have an umbrella. There would be no point in arguing with her—not that I ever have—because she'd be right.

I've enjoyed dinner, despite Jack's statement earlier in the evening. It was just like old times, minus the pressure of having to write a paper and greasy pizza. Tonight reminded me of *why* we're friends. We get along so well, and whenever I'm around him I feel relaxed—although that took a moment to come back—and like I can be myself because I know he wouldn't judge me.

It's part of the reason why I fell for him.

Jack leans down, his voice straining to be heard over the downpour, pulling me from my thoughts. "Have you ever danced in the rain?"

My eyes dart to him, widening at the absurdity of his question. What sort of crazy person does that? It only works in the movies and that's because the rain is actually warm water and they aren't likely to catch a cold.

"Do you even know me?"

Jack laughs, before a warm, slightly calloused hand takes the one not holding my purse, and before I know it, I'm being dragged into the freezing cold rainfall. Within seconds, my fitted black mini dress is drenched and my carefully curled hair is plastered to my forehead. The slight sting of my mascara running into my eyes has me tugging on Jack's hand as I shout, "What are you doing?"

He doesn't let go. Instead, he shouts over his shoulder, a big grin on his face, "Living a little."

A shiver travels down my spine as a gust of wind blows through the buildings. The first thing that pops into my head rolls out of my mouth before I can stop it. "But we're getting wet."

Duh.

Jack laughs, tugging my hand until I stumble into him. We're standing in the middle of the street but there's not a car in sight. It's just the two of us in the rain, under the white glow of the street lamp, everyone else sane enough to stay dry inside. One arm wraps around my waist, pulling me close, as he repositions the one still holding my hand. In the warmth of his arms, I don't feel so cold anymore.

I feel like the girl in the movie who gets the guy.

Except I know I won't.

Leaning down, Jack murmurs in my ear, "We can't change it, so we might as well embrace it."

He has a point. It's not like stepping back under the ease will miraculously make us dry. But then again, I'd still be dry if he didn't pull me into the rain. I guess it depends which side of the coin you look at.

Jack starts swaying, forcing my body to move with his. When he dips his head again, I hold my breath. "Loosen up, Sutton. Just enjoy the dance."

I turn my head, our mouths so close and yet so far. Even to my own ears, my voice sounds breathy as I say, "But there's no music."

I'm not sure what I expect, perhaps for Jack to laugh again at my second obvious statement in a matter of minutes or for him to release me and send me on my way for being no fun. I certainly don't expect him to start humming a song.

Resting my head on his shoulder, I close my eyes, inhaling the clean citrus scent of his aftershave mixed with the freshness of the rain. I allow the drinks I had with dinner to let my guard down as I relax into his body. The vibrations of his chest as he hums provide an odd sort of comfort and even though he isn't singing any words, it sounds kind of familiar. "What song is that?"

"*The Night We Met* by Lord Huron."

I want to ask him why he chose that song, but I also don't want to ruin the moment. With the rain falling on us and the unusual quiet to a normally bustling city, I can pretend that the man holding me in his arms wants more.

I can pretend that we can *be* more.

Pushing me out, I swirl away from him, the puddles of rain splashing on my bare legs before I'm tugged back into him. I fall into his solid chest with a gasp at the feel of his hard body against mine. There's a heated charge of energy between us. It's been there all night, but I push it away *again*, certain that my mind, soul, and body are luring me into a false sense of security. I'm projecting the feelings I had back in college.

That's all it is.

When he finishes the song, I lift my chin, only now realizing that the rain has stopped. Jack's eyes search mine, looking for something as his hold on me tightens. When he lifts a hand to smooth back the soaked strands of my hair, my lips part and struggle to pull in much needed air.

The distant sound of traffic becomes muted as I look up at him with bated breath. His gaze fills with a hot and electric look, something I never thought I'd see from him, of all people. I'm questioning my whole existence as a fire of desire sparks to life in the pit of my stomach.

Please don't let him see anything reflected in my eyes.

All I can do is lean into his solid frame as I blink up at him, powerless as he closes the distance between us. His large hands cup my face as he smooths his thumbs over the apples of my cheeks.

"May I?"

My brow furrows as my mind works at double speed through the fog, trying to process the question. I can't connect the dots on what exactly he's asking for. Without fully understanding what I'm agreeing to, I find myself nodding anyway.

At a slight incline, Jack dips his head, brushing his lips over mine. It's the barest of touches and yet my pussy throbs, warmth spreading out and consuming me.

I need more.

Jack pulls away a fraction, his eyes searching mine again. Water clings to his lashes and I watch a single droplet roll down his cheek to the corner of his mouth. I'm vaguely aware of my hand grabbing onto the damp cotton of his shirt. I don't know if I'm holding on to anchor myself or silently asking for more.

The ghost of his lips still on my own has the breath catching in my throat. I can't breathe and yet I feel alive. My mind is a jumble of thoughts that I can't put into order. Jack dips his head again, dusting his lips over mine once more. This time when he pulls away, there's barely half an inch between our mouths. I know that if I could formulate words, our lips would touch just from the movement.

It feels like an eternity with us standing in the middle of the road, Jack cupping my face and me holding onto his shirt. I can smell the whiskey on his breath and briefly, I wonder if he can smell the gin on mine. I want to taste the whiskey on his tongue. To make him feel half as consumed by me as I am with him.

My name leaves his lips, pained and yet desperate, before he crushes his mouth to mine. This kiss is nothing like the two before. It's dominating and possessive, sending a jolt through my body. Jack's hands leave my face, one traveling into my hair as the other grips my hip.

I've never felt this electrified by a kiss before.

It's powerful and all-consuming. I don't want this kiss to end, I want to make it last a lifetime. In this moment, I know what people mean when they talk about someone being their 'home'.

The thought sobers me slightly, at least enough to realize what we're doing. Flattening my hand to his chest, I push away, needing a moment to breathe. Jack's hands leave my body and I instantly miss the contact. I need to get my mind in order and figure out what I want.

Him. It's always been him.

At this very moment, I know I can either walk away and never experience all that we could be, or I can take what he's offering and know that it's all I'll probably ever get of him.

My breaths come in ragged gasps, the rain long

forgotten as I look at the man who's owned my heart for as long as I can remember. There's no other option. I'll always wonder what if and I'm tired of living my life to please other people. *This is for me.*

My voice sounds thick when I say, "Take me home."

Something akin to disappointment etches its way across his handsome face before he drops his head. When he lifts it again, it's gone, a mask in place before he nods and shrugs out of his jacket.

Oh God, I hope I haven't read this wrong.

I pull in a breath, hyping myself up for what I need to say. When he wraps his jacket around my shoulders, my hand lands on his, forcing his focus to me. "To your home, Jack."

NINE

Jack

I've got to be dreaming. It's like all my birthdays and Christmases have come at once. I practically drag Sutton to find a cab the moment she confirms that she wants to go back to my place.

My heart beats an unsteady rhythm in my chest, giddy at what's to come. As much as I want this to happen, if she changes her mind, I'll stop. But for now, I'm going to try and savor every moment.

That's easier said than done, especially since I haven't let her up for air since we stepped out of the cab. I use muscle memory to tap in the code, pushing open my front door with one hand as I hold on to her slender waist with the other.

Is this real?

How am I, Jack O'Riley, kissing Sutton Quinn?

If it wasn't for the amplified feelings rushing through my body, I'd think this was a figment of my imagination.

I'm still expecting to snap back to reality any minute now.

I knew the moment I picked her up at her hotel that I was done for. I've tried all evening to play it cool, act like tonight isn't a big deal, and that this energy I feel pulsing beneath the surface is nothing.

All I want is to make her happy, for her to know that whenever she steps into a room, the tension seeps out of my body. And yet, I know that if I told her this, especially when she's so stiff and guarded, I'll scare her away. So, I did what any sane man would do. I shrugged off her questions and tried like hell to get her to relax.

And it worked. But the second I pulled her into my arms in the rain, I knew I couldn't pretend I wasn't affected anymore. One brush of my lips over hers and it was like a current passing through me, bringing my body and soul to life.

I need more.

I need everything from her. *Forever*.

Pushing open the door, I guide Sutton in, pressing her against the wall of the hallway. The lights flicker on at the movement and the alarm beeps. *Thank God, I never sold my place*. I pull away, showing my face to the control panel next to the door, before kicking it shut. When the sound of the alarm switching off echoes around the apartment, my eyes land back on her.

Sutton's chest heaves, matching my own as we stand inches away from each other, but not touching. I want to take a step forward, pick up where we left off, but I also don't want to rush her.

If she decides to only give me tonight—because let's face it, I'll be a lucky asshole to get even that much—I want to be haunted by images of us together in this house. I know that there's nobody else out there for me. It's always been her.

My voice is hoarse as I lift my hand to cup her face and say, "Sutton."

A whimper leaves her lips and I close the distance between us, my mouth falling on hers with an urgency that she mirrors.

Somewhere through the lust that is clouding my mind, the rational side calls, urging me to take a step back. I need to get my thoughts in order or I'll drown, blow my load, and fuck this up. This might be the beginning of the end for us if I do.

Sutton's hand reaches out, resting on my bicep as I take a step back, then another. Her body follows me and my brows tug together at the look of hurt and confusion swirling in her brown eyes.

Shit, what've I done?

Have I forced myself on her?

Did she not want—

"If you've changed your mind, I can le—"

Fuck no. I don't let her finish that sentence.

Whatever she was about to say is not happening, and I refuse to allow her to speak it into existence. My hands slide into the damp strands of her hair, tugging her head back almost too forcefully before I silence her with my mouth. Any thought of slowing this down or taking a moment to get my head together is long forgotten.

Her moans are like music to my ears as we stumble down the hallway. The crash of something smashing on the floor barely penetrates the haze I'm in. She's like a drug I can't get enough of.

When we reach the bottom of the stairs, I pull my mouth away from Sutton's. Her fingers flex in the fabric of my shirt and our labored breaths fill the quiet of the house. Taking her hand, I lead the way upstairs to my bedroom, barely resisting the urge to pinch myself.

Neither of us speaks. Surely she won't be unsure of how much I want her now? I can feel her trembling where we're connected and I'm certain it's not from the chill of the air conditioning and her rain-soaked clothes.

We reach my room, but I hesitate for a moment. Maybe I should take us to one of the spare bedrooms. Christ, maybe I shouldn't have brought us to the house, full stop. In all my years of dating, I've never once questioned whether or not I should bring a woman into my space. But with Sutton, I want to make a good impression.

Turning to face her, I pull in a breath. "Don't judge me, okay?"

Her brows tug together, and she tilts her head. "Why would I judge you?"

Sighing, I reply, "When I came to London originally, I wasn't sociable and basically locked myself in the lab in the basement and 'tinkered' as my mom would say. I put a few things on display and now my house looks like a shrine to fucking *Tony Stark*. I…"

Sutton rolls her lips before they spread into a wide grin. I can't help but return it, stepping into her space as I rest my forehead on hers. "I said don't judge me."

"I'm not. I think it's cute and… kinda sexy."

"Yeah?"

She nods, glancing down at where our chests meet before looking into my eyes. "Yeah. Maybe you can show me your collection later?"

Hell yes.

Without a word, I tug Sutton into my room and to the bathroom. I let go of her hand to turn on the shower and when I turn around, she's standing in the middle of the room, her arms folded as she rubs her palms over her exposed skin.

The overhead lights let me see her in all her glory. Even with mascara tracks on her cheeks and her hair wet and messy, she's still the most beautiful woman I've ever seen. I don't miss how her eyes are wide and slightly disbelieving. Like she too can't quite believe this is happening.

Stepping toward her, I remove my jacket from her shoulders, throwing it into one of the sinks. My attention's drawn to the hard buds of her nipples protruding through her dress. I want to touch and taste them, but I need to get her warmed up first.

Steam fills the room and the patter of water falling

on the tile is the only noise around us as we continue to stare at each other. Taking a step back, I slowly unbutton my shirt, pulling it off and throwing it in the direction of my jacket. Fumbling, my fingers find the hem of my undershirt, tugging it over my head, leaving me in only my jeans. Running a hand through my hair, I hold my breath as Sutton moves forward, her hand hovering over my stomach. Questioning eyes look up at me and in answer, I cover her hand with mine, bringing it forward until she's touching my skin. A wave of chemistry crashes into me, pulling me under.

Sutton sucks in a breath as I exhale one in a hiss at the contact. Her delicate hands trace over my abs. I want to know what she's thinking. *Is she as turned on as I am? Does she find me attractive?*

I know I'm not as jacked as Noah. *Does she want me like she wanted him?* Christ, where is this coming from? I'm not the same gangly kid I was ten years ago. I've worked hard on my physique and although I might not be as handsome or buff as Noah, I can hold my own.

Sutton's fingers go lower, resting on my belt buckle. "Jack?"

Focus. You're going to mess this up.

Smoothing back a hair that's stuck to her cheek, I cup her face and force my insecurities away. "Yeah, baby?"

She swallows, nuzzling into my palm, and when she closes her eyes a knot of worry forms in the pit of my stomach. *So much for pushing them away.* Is she going to let me down? Tell me that she's changed her mind? Or worse yet, that I should know better than to think I have a shot with her?

Christ, I already know she's too good for me.

Brown eyes look up at me, and I see nothing but arousal swirling in the depths. Her voice is thick when she asks, "Why aren't you undressing me?"

I drag my teeth over my bottom lip, pulling it into my mouth as I contemplate my next move. Fuck, if I'm not on cloud nine now. Sutton's question doesn't need an answer with words, it needs action.

My hands land on her waist, and I tug her into me. Her eyes flutter closed as a sexy moan falls from her lips. There's no denying my attraction to her, not with the way my cock is prodding into her stomach. My fingers find the zipper of her dress, tugging it down as I nuzzle her neck.

She smells like a floral bouquet with a hint of sweetness, and I groan, knowing she'll taste as good as she smells. Pulling away, her dress falls to her waist and I smooth my hands over her hips as I push it down and then help her step from it.

The sight before me is mesmerizing. She's in a black lacy G-string and matching strapless bra. Her stomach is toned when I bend down to help her remove her shoes I can't help but roam my hands over every inch of her body.

Sutton's pussy is level with my eyes, with only the thin fabric of her panties between us. It would be so easy to lean forward and bury my nose into her folds, but I'm not sure I could stop at that. I want to taste her. To imprint her scent into the fabric of my skin in the most animalistic way possible.

Calming the caveman inside of me, I help Sutton out of her shoes, moving them and her dress to the side before I stand. I drop my eyes to my belt as I pull it through the loops, focusing on the task at hand.

Shower, then I can worship her body. In that order.

Repeating the words over and over, I push my soaked jeans down my legs before kicking them to the side. When I go to grab Sutton's hand, I come up empty, a frown tugging on my brows as I turn to face her with a question on the tip of my tongue.

A knowing smirk lifts the corner of her mouth as she says, "I don't know about you, Jack, but when I get in the shower, I don't wear clothes."

Scrubbing a hand over the back of my neck, I reply, "I know, but I figured yo..."

The words die on my lips as Sutton reaches behind her and unclasps her bra. She drops it to the floor and my eyes fall to the full globes of her breasts. They're perky and fucking perfect, just like I would've expected. Dusky pink nipples point at me, begging to be sucked on.

Like a horny schoolboy, I'm so distracted by her breasts and the things I want to do to them that I miss the fact she's removed her G-string. Sutton squeezes past me into the walk-in shower, her chest brushing me as she passes. Her voice is thick and full of arousal when she says, "Hurry up, Jack."

Springing into action, I remove my black boxer briefs, tripping over my feet as I try to step free. My cock springs out and up, hitting me in the stomach. *It fucking hurts.*

Sutton chuckles, drawing my attention to her and distracting me from the pain. "Careful. You'll ruin the evening if we have to end up in the ER."

Playing it cool—or as cool as a guy can when he nearly fell flat on his face—I shrug. "I meant to do that. It's a little trick I'm perfecting."

Her brows lift as she says, "Right."

Sutton steps further under the water as I walk into the shower. Her eyes are closed as she pushes her hands through her hair. The water is raining down on her, much like it did earlier in the evening, except this time, I can see all of her. She's relaxed and loose—there's no guard being put up or show being put on. This is her and I love that *I* get to see this side of her when she shows it to so few people. I take a moment to admire the curves of her body, pinching the skin on my thigh to make sure this is real.

When her eyes open, she looks at me, her mouth opening a fraction and her irises becoming impossibly dark. That look, coming from her, fills me with confidence and I stalk toward her. White teeth dig into the plumpness of her bottom lip, the delicate skin going pale with the pressure. My thumb swipes over her lip, releasing it.

I don't give her a second to think, my mouth descends on hers, taking everything she'll give me.

Bending my legs, I wrap my hands around the back of her thighs and lift her. Instinctively, her legs wrap around my waist and I press her into the wall.

My tongue demands entry, and she gives it willingly. It's not a perfect kiss, but because it's her, it is. I don't know what I did to get so lucky, but I'm going to make her feel so good. I'm going to make sure this is the best night of her life.

I'm going to show her that I can be everything she's ever needed in a partner, that she can be proud to have me on her arm.

Leaving her lips, I can't help but feel a sense of pride at the way she gasps in breaths and moans my name. Moving down the column of her throat, I kiss and nip at the sensitive flesh until I reach my destination. I latch my mouth onto her nipple, swirling my tongue around the bud before grazing it with my teeth and then sucking on it hard.

I repeat the action a couple of times before switching to the next; her moans urging me on. All the while, Sutton's head is thrown back, and she's rocking her hips into me, looking for her release.

It would be so easy to slip into her, the wetness she's leaving on me a sure sign that she's ready. I refuse to let our first time be against the wall of my shower. Sure, we'll have a lot of first times but our first, first time is going to be done properly and in my bed.

Gentle fingers dive into my hair, pulling my head

away from my new favorite place. "Jack, I need you, now."

It's like music to my ears. I turn from the wall, ready to carry Sutton to my bed. My mind is focused on getting her there, regardless of the impracticalities given our naked, wet bodies.

Her voice is light and I feel the vibrations of laughter as she calls, "Jack. The shower. We need to switch it off."

Fuck. I'm so fucked.

I continue into the bedroom, calling, "Marley, turn off the shower."

A three-second tune plays out, signifying the command has been actioned.

Sutton's eyes widen, and she swallows, biting down on her bottom lip. "That's my... You didn't switch it on like that."

Crap. It didn't even cross my mind. She was never supposed to be in this house, so I figured why not have a constant reminder of the woman I'm in love with but can't have? I need to do some serious damage control. *What was I thinking giving my home system her middle name?* I wasn't. And that's the problem.

Taking a seat on the edge of the bed with Sutton straddling my lap and my painfully hard cock firmly wedged between us, I reply, "It's a fully customizable dual system. You can name it whatever you like, and it does both voice command and button controls." I pause, searching for the right words, but none come to me. "I... don't know what to say."

Sutton nods as if she understands. I don't think she does. How can she? She's perfect and could have any guy she wants and yet here she is, in my lap, naked and calm as ever about the fact that I named my home system after her. Anyone else would run a mile.

She rolls her hips, her voice quiet and reassuring when she says, "Tell me what you want."

I'm not sure she's ready for that.

If naming my home system after her doesn't scare her away, then telling her I want to marry her, fill her with my babies, and keep her here in my arms for eternity sure will.

Instead, I take her lack of shock as a good sign and pick up where we left off. "I want you to sit on my face and ride it until I tell you that you can stop."

Sutton's eyes widen a fraction before she nods and pushes me onto my back. She crawls up my body, looking into my eyes, before she pulls in a breath and hovers over my face. When I wrap my hands around her thighs and pull her down, I feel resistance.

My words come out as a growl, frustration at being so close to her pussy and yet so far. "Sit, Sutton. You're fucking hovering."

Our eyes connect, a silent argument taking place before she realizes she won't win, and sighs, dropping down, covering my mouth with her pussy. I'm greedy and desperate, feasting on her like I'll never get enough. She tastes sweet and even better than I could have imagined. I lap her up, alternating between swirling my tongue around her clit and fucking her with it.

The only disadvantage to having her sit on my face is the fact that I can't have her ride my fingers. *I guess we have all night for that.* Sutton's moans urge me on. Her fingers dive into my hair, tugging on the strands as she groans and begs me for more, bucking her hips as she seeks out her release.

Her voice is breathy, sending jolts of desire to my cock as she screams, "Jack, I'm gonna come."

Sutton trembles and I move my hands from her thighs over her toned stomach and up to her breasts. They fit like perfection in my palms and I massage the full globes, in part to keep her upright but also to increase her pleasure. My fingers roll the tight buds of her nipples and she covers my hands with her own, increasing the pressure.

Her thighs squeeze the sides of my head and I drive my tongue into her tight hole, drinking down every drop of her cum. She collapses forward, before rolling off of my face to lie beside me. The sound of her labored breathing fills the room and I look over at her, a cocky grin that I can't hold back, spreading over my face.

Her hand gently slaps at my shoulder, her face softening into a dazed smile as she says, "Don't look at me like that."

Rolling onto my front, I climb up her body, hovering over her, as I ask, "Like what?"

Sutton rests her hands on my chest, a seriousness

falling over us as she skates them down. With a voice filled with lust, she wraps her hand around my cock stroking it slowly as she says, "Like you're 'the man'."

My breath rushes out of me. I don't feel like 'the man' right now. I feel like her captive and whatever she asks of me, I'll do. Clearing my throat, I will myself to stay strong and remember that this isn't about my pleasure—that comes later—this is about hers. I've had hand jobs before, but they've never robbed me of the ability to think.

"What's wrong, Jack? Cat got your tongue?"

Dropping down, I halt her movements, trapping her hand between our bodies.

My pride is doing all the talking when I ask, "Tell me, have you ever orgasmed that hard with another man?"

Screw the fact that she could dent my ego by telling me that she's come harder, a sick part of me needs to know. If she tells me yes, I'll keep practicing until I'm the one that makes her come the hardest. Until she's as addicted to me as I'm becoming to her in a whole new way.

With her free hand, she smooths back the hair that's hanging over my brow. A soft look takes over her face and her eyes fill with sincerity when she replies, "I've never orgasmed that hard with another man. Or sat on his face like that."

Good.

TEN

Sutton

An involuntary groan slips free when Jack stands from the bed. My body moves with him as I lift onto my elbows. Greedily, my eyes roam over his body. *How is he so perfect?* He's not bulky but instead athletic in his build. Soft abs lead down to a perfect, hard cock and I lick my lips, eager to taste him.

Some might say it's average, but to me, it's the best one I've ever seen. A good six and a half inches—if I had to guess—and thick enough that I can barely touch my fingertips together.

He walks to the bedside table, opens the drawer, and takes something out. When he chucks it on the bed, the foil of the condoms catches the dim light of the lamp in the corner of the room. My focus is on them until the sound of a packet tearing pulls my attention back to him and I watch as he sheaths his cock.

I feel like I might wake up and realize this is all a dream. Any moment now, I'll open my eyes in my bedroom, back in New York, the sound of my alarm blaring through my room. I'll be alone, my body tense and wired from the lack of fulfillment. Like it usually is when I dream of him.

With the condom on, Jack crawls up my body, dragging his nose along my skin. It feels so real, a trail of goosebumps following behind him. Tilting my head back, I arch my back, pushing my chest in his direction.

A dark chuckle falls from his lips and I know he understands what I'm asking for. Especially when his mouth latches onto my nipple. The feel of his tongue swirling around the tight bud makes me moan and grip his hair to hold him in place.

More.

The word repeats in my mind like a chant. I don't know what's happening to me, but I feel... alive and almost over stimulated. It's like there's a charge pulsating through my body and I just want to find a release, despite having had one moments ago.

His cock rests at the entrance of my pussy. A desire to have him take the condom off has me biting my tongue and swallowing down the words. I need to remember this is a one-time thing. *A natural continuation of our date.* We're just two adults satisfying our most basic of needs.

Jack lifts his head, the pop of his mouth leaving my nipple echoes around the room. He dusts kisses across my chest, moving up the expanse of my throat. When he reaches my lips, he brushes the faintest of kisses over them.

Moaning, I tell him, "Jack, I need more. Now."

Of what? Him, but I'll settle for kisses, orgasms, his body on mine. I'll take anything he's willing to give. Consequences be damned.

I grip his hips, pulling his lower body closer. The action has the head of his cock pressing into my entrance. It's a delicious feeling and one I want to savor because I'm about to experience *him* in a way I thought would never happen. I feel breathless and *whole*. Through the mental fuzziness, a clarifying thought bursts in. This is the most right thing I will ever do. *I'll never regret him.*

Jack's lips press against mine before his tongue demands entry. I give it up freely, embracing the intimacy that comes with loving another person.

Our tongues tangle and I moan as he eases in, stretching me with his cock in the most satisfying way possible. This is what I've wanted. It feels like duvet days on a cold rainy day. Like my favorite comfort food when I'm feeling down. This is *love*.

No, Sutton. This isn't anything like that.

This is just sex.

Nothing more.

Jack pushes in and our combined groans fill the room, reverberating off the walls and back to us. When he's fully seated, he wraps an arm around my waist, rolling us until he's on his back and I'm on top. I push up so I'm sitting on him, tipping my head back as I revel in the sensation of having him so much deeper. The curve of his cock hits a spot I'm not sure anyone else has ever reached.

When his hands grip my hips, I give a tentative roll, testing out the position. Jack's eyes are dark and stormy as he looks up at me. There's a lot being said in the blue of his gaze. It gives me the confidence to increase my pace.

Resting my hands on his chest, I moan at the feeling of him inside of me. "Mmm, that feels so good."

His teeth are clenched when he hisses, "I'm gonna need you to ride me harder, Sutton. Take everything that you need and get yourself off on my cock, baby."

Without needing to be told twice, I roll and twist my hips as I seek my release. Jack has a hand on my hip, his fingers tensing and releasing the flesh, letting me know that he's enjoying the movements.

When his hand reaches up and holds onto my breast, I cover it with mine, urging him to squeeze and massage the flesh. It's too much and I'm going to come too soon. I don't want this to be over yet. I'm not ready for reality to burst our bubble because I know it will.

"Jack, I need—" My words trail off, the pleasure building inside of me as my hips keep up the momentum. With my eyes closed and my head tipped back, I try to clear through the fog of lust that's consuming me. It's so hard when he fits *so* well.

His voice comes out gruff, drawing my heady gaze to him. "What do you need? Talk to me."

You.

The word pops into my mind, nearly tumbling from my lips unchecked. Catching myself, I dash it away, instead saying, "I need to come." But *I don't want this to end*, is left unsaid.

Jack nods, flipping me onto my back before he pulls out. My whimper at the loss has a confident smirk lifting the corner of his mouth. He shuffles down my body until he's between my legs and then his hot mouth is covering my pussy and the loss of contact is forgotten. Pushing my thighs, he spreads me wider, tongue fucking me. I swear he has a magic tongue. The way he swirls it around as his teeth graze over my clit is too much.

Blood rushes to my pussy, the walls spasming around air as I climb the apex of my release. My heartbeat sounds in my ears and I lose all feeling in my legs as I enter a state of euphoria. A wave of what I can only describe as happiness and contentment washes over me as I cry out my release. He's right there, lapping me up like he's been deprived of my cum his entire life.

Jack's name tumbles from my lips over and over again. I shriek when he flips me onto my stomach, lifts my hips, and drives into me with enough force to set off another orgasm. His hips jerk as he pistons into me, the grunts and groans falling from his lips are animalistic and turn me on more than I ever could have imagined.

Thrusting his hips, Jack's moans fill my ears. I don't

know that I'll ever forget what he sounds like when he's racing toward his release. It's guttural and all man. His body tenses, and with a gasp he comes, his body jerking as he fills the condom.

When he's finished, he pulls my body close and collapses us onto the bed. Our breathing is loud in the otherwise quiet house and I luxuriate in the feeling, keeping reality on the outside of the bubble we're in.

I know he's going to need to get up soon, remove the condom, and then we'll need to figure out what happens next, but that can wait. Turning my head, our eyes hold contact, a soft sleepy smile on his lips. Jack pulls back his hips and I feel the loss of him inside my pussy and my heart.

Maybe this doesn't have to be a one-time thing.

It would be so easy to say 'I love you'. My body tenses at the thought of the words accidentally spilling from my mouth. *This is too intimate for a casual hook up. Which is exactly what he said this was. Right?*

Unable to stand the confusion of my thoughts, I look away, preparing to stand from the bed and get my clothes to leave. If I stay, I'm liable to say something that I shouldn't.

Jack's arm wraps around me, pulling me into his body. He places a gentle kiss on my shoulder, murmuring into my skin, "I'm going to get rid of this condom. When I come back, you're going to be under the covers because I'm not done with you."

ELEVEN

Sutton

The summer sun spills through the open blinds, a beam casting across the mattress and reflecting a prism of light onto the wall opposite. It's a huge contrast to the downpour we experienced yesterday. I lie in the light, basking in its warmth before my brows pull into a frown, my mind registering the delicious ache throughout my body. The events of last night replay like a movie.

Oh God.

What was I thinking coming back to his place and doing what we did?

Was it the best sex of my life? Yes. Do I want more? Without a doubt. Should I get the hell out of here? Most certainly.

Turning toward Jack, I let my eyes freely roam. The sheet barely covers him, resting low on his hips. I can see the outline of his cock and the urge to touch him, to take him into my mouth, is almost too much.

Should I stay and see what happens?

It might be awkward. Or it could lead to more of last night. I bite my bottom lip, thinking over my options before the clock on the bedside table catches my eye.

It's seven thirty, which means my flight's in just over five hours. I need to get to the hotel, pack my things, and get to the airport. *Crap*. And I need to email the contract to Lord Pendleton. I knew I should have done it yesterday after the meeting but I was too amped up for dinner that I focused on getting ready. As much as I want to stay here and close my eyes as I snuggle into Jack, I don't have the time. *And that's not my reality.*

Dragging my eyes away from him, I climb from the bed, tip toeing into the bathroom. *Please, lights, don't come on.* The overhead light flickers on, illuminating my sexed up state in the mirror. Turning my back on my reflection, I swipe up my dress, pulling it up my body before dropping it when the still damp fabric touches my skin.

Cracking open the bathroom door, I send up a silent prayer that the light doesn't wake him. Closing the door behind me, I dart across the room and into his closet. I feel like a thief. On a mission, I move to the drawers, pulling them open and snatching up a t-shirt. It's baggy and will cover me enough to take a cab from here back to my hotel. I'll return it in the city. If we see each other again.

I can think about it later.

I can think about the past twenty-four hours later. Right now my focus needs to be on getting to the airport and not missing my flight. *And sending that email.* I can't believe he's had me so consumed.

Pulling in a breath, I open the closet door and move through his bedroom, down the hallway and stairs. Finally, I allow myself to take one last look at his home. *His sanctuary.* Classic comics in poster frames hang from the walls and I can't help but smile at them. It's classic Jack. At heart, he's a smart, brilliant, and yet nerdy guy.

A creak from above makes me jump and I swipe up my purse from where I dropped it by the front door. *God, I hope his door opens.* Rooting around inside, I pull out my phone. *Okay, five percent charge.* That should get me an Uber back to the hotel. I move through the motions of ordering the car before tackling the door.

This isn't me running away. Okay, maybe it's a little bit of me running away. I have a meeting in New York this evening. I *have* to be on this flight. But I won't lie to myself. I need some time to process what happened last night and come up with a plan on how to face Jack again without it being awkward. I want his friendship, even if I have nothing else to offer him.

Distracted, I climb into the back of the Uber. The feel of Jack's lips, hands, and cock like a ghost haunting my skin. How long will I feel like this? Bereft of his contact and craving more of him that I know I'll never get.

Holding the phone between my ear and shoulder, I listen to the international dial tone, waiting for Minnie to pick up. I've just got in from my meeting with the Saudi prince.

My shoulders are tense with the stress of the day weighing me down. Despite my scratchy eyes and heavy limbs, I'm determined to enjoy my glass of wine and sink into the couch cushions.

"Darling," Minnie exclaims when she picks up. "Guess who's back in the city next week?"

For the first time since returning from London, a genuine smile lifts at the corner of my mouth. I put my wineglass on the coffee table in front of me before replying, "Would that be you, by any chance?"

"Got it in one. I knew you would. You always were such an A-plus student. How are you?"

I gnaw at my bottom lip as I fiddle with my necklace. There's a reluctance to tell Minnie the reason for my call. She'll undoubtedly be ecstatic at the fact that *something* happened between me and Jack. I know she'll also understand when I tell her how conflicted I am about what to do next.

"Something happened in London."

Minnie goes quiet and when I'm not forthcoming with more, she softly asks, "What happened, Sutton?"

Here goes nothing. "Well, you know how I told you a while ago that I felt like I was being watched?"

"Of course. You refused to go to the police."

I brush off her comment because now that I know it was Jack, I'm glad I didn't file a report. "It turns out it was Jack. He followed me to London and asked me out to dinner."

Minnie gasps and I can just picture her resting her hand on her collarbone. "Please tell me you went?"

A chuckle falls from my lips because that's just like Minnie. She's always been an advocate for me and Jack. He could do no wrong in her eyes—including stalking me, apparently. "Yes. We went to dinner. And then back to his place."

I let the words hang in the air and when they finally register for her she lets out a squeal that has me pulling the phone away from my ear. Her giddiness is infectious and I find myself smiling despite my feelings when I woke up in his bed. When I can no longer hear her shrieking, I bring the phone back.

"Sutton, I am going to need you to give me all of the details. I don't care how explicit they are."

Laughing, I tease, "You should know me better than that. I don't kiss and tell, Minnie." I pause, sobering before continuing, "But I do need your help."

"First of all, that's very selfish of you. You're the first person I'd call after a tantalizing night with a hottie like Jack. What do you need my help with? I can lend you my copy of the *Karma Sutra,* but the last time I tried you blushed to high heaven."

Jack doesn't need *any* directions from me in the bedroom.

Pulling in a breath, I force myself back to the present, swiping my palm down the front of my navy summer dress. Now isn't the time to be getting all hot and bothered over memories of how he touched, teased, and tasted me.

Knowing Minnie like I do, I rush out my next words, not giving her the chance to interrupt. "I left when he was still asleep. I had to catch my flight, but I also just needed some space because I don't know how to handle the change in our dynamic. Because it will change. What we did isn't something you can pretend didn't happen."

When I'm finished, I blow out a breath, my shoulders sagging with relief. If I couldn't hear the background noise on her end, I would have thought we'd lost our connection.

"Okay. That's a lot to unpack. I guess the first question you need to ask yourself is what do you want? Because you can either tell him it meant nothing and brush it under the carpet like a sordid affair or tell him you want to explore the relationship and give the two of you a real shot."

The conversation with Jack at dinner when I asked him why he asked me out replays in my mind like a siren warning me of danger. I gave him two opportunities to tell me why and he played it down both times. That's not something I can ignore.

My voice comes out as a croak when I finally speak. "He said it was just a casual exploration."

Minnie tsks before asking, "Has he tried to reach out since you left?"

I wince at her question. Jack hasn't tried to reach out and as much as I keep telling myself he's probably busy, the reality is a whole day has nearly passed across two timezones. My voice is small and foreign to my ears when I reply, "No. Not a word."

Sighing, Minnie's voice is soothing and filled with sympathy when she says, "I think that tells you all you need to know, Sutton. I'm so sorry, honey."

She's right. His lack of contact added to his determination that last night was nothing to look too much into should be all the clarity I need. Still, I know that I'm going to have to call him and get the closure I need.

A knock at the door pulls me from my thoughts. My brows pull together and I twist my wrist to check the time. It must be Ms. Wilson after some milk again. She always seems to run out during the week and knocks on all the doors until she finds someone to give her some.

"I've got to go, Minnie. Someone's at the door. I'll call you later."

Minnie calls out a goodbye and I disconnect the call, throwing my phone on the couch as I stand and make my way through the apartment.

TWELVE

Jack

W aking up alone was not how I imagined my morning starting, especially after the night we shared. Finding out the woman I'm head over heels in love with had jumped on a flight and left the country was the icing on the cake, or in my case the banana to my pudding.

My knee bounces as I wait for my flight to be called. I've paid a little over four figures for this last-minute flight, but it'll get me back to New York quicker than a private jet. It's money well spent and time is of the essence.

The speaker announces another flight that's ready to board and I internally curse at the fact that mine hasn't been called yet. It's not like it's delayed, so my frustration is unwarranted, but I can't calm the anxiety clawing at my throat.

An energy I've never felt before buzzes through my body. It's different from the kind I felt last night or the one I experienced when I first figured out how to get Home to integrate every facet of someone's home without bogging down their Wi-Fi or requiring expensive replacement equipment. This one is nervous and unsure, yet buzzing with excitement.

Standing, I pace the area in front of the seats, with my hands on my hips and my eyes occasionally darting to the board above the gate. There's nobody manning the desk, and watching it isn't going to make someone appear or time speed up.

A gentle hand rests on my arm. I turn, looking down into a set of weathered blue eyes. A Bostonian accent admonishes, "You're making me nervous with all this pacing."

"Sorry," I mumble, scrubbing my hand over the back of my neck. "I'm just a little desperate to get home."

"Why don't you come and tell us all about it?" The gentleman looks back at a woman sitting forward in her seat. Intense eyes watching me, with a soft smile on her face.

Maybe it's the distraction I need, plus it can't hurt to get this off my chest. It's not like I can call someone up to vent, not with the fact that my phone died the moment I went through security. I've been so focused on getting on this flight that it's not even crossed my mind to find a charger and I'm not going to now, given the flight could board any minute. *I'm a mess.*

It can only help, that's why I find myself replying, "Sure." I follow him over to the lady I assume is his wife, taking a seat but keeping one eye on the gate even as he makes the introductions.

"This is Lucy, my wife, and I'm Alfred. Why don't you tell us what has you all pent up?"

Exhaling, I ask, "Where to start?"

Lucy's voice is soft, and she rests her frail hand on my arm like she's worried about scaring me away. "At the beginning is usually a good place."

I spill my guts to Alfred and Lucy, berating myself throughout as I tell them the story of how Sutton and I met thirteen years ago, in the back of a communications lecture. Reliving the memories only serves to remind me of the fact that she's the woman for me. I see everything in a different light, including the night she came to my party four years ago.

How did I miss the signs?

I could feel her eyes on me the entire night as I worked the room. And now that I think back, there was a hint of disappointment in her gaze when I asked Noah to keep her company.

Fuck, I'm an idiot.

We could have been something all this time. I all but pushed her into my best friend's arms, and after last night and waking up alone, I might never get her back. *Not that I had her in the first place.* My chest aches at the revelation, a heaviness settling in that I'm not sure I'll ever get rid of if I lose her.

Raising my fist, I knock on Sutton's apartment door, willing the nervous energy inside of me to calm down. It feels like an eternity before she swings the door open. I don't miss the way the surprise registers on her face before she shuts it down. The mask she uses for everyone else coming into full force.

For a moment, I wonder if I've made a mistake. *Should I have given her a couple of days to get used to the idea of what we did?* I should have. God, I was so focused on proving to myself that I'm good enough for her now, that I didn't even consider that she might not want me anyway. I might have billions in my bank account, but does that even matter to her? I don't think so.

Uncertainty fills Sutton's voice when she asks, "Jack, what are you doing here?"

Shoving my hands into the pockets of my jeans, I rock forward on my feet, nervous at what's to come. I want to be near her, to touch her and yet, the way she's half hiding behind the door, tells me she doesn't want that too. "You ran out on me."

Sutton hesitates, looking away before meeting my eyes. "I had a flight to catch."

Frustration coats my words. "Right, and you couldn't wake me?"

She at least has the sense to look sheepish when she

replies, "It didn't cross my mind." Her brows tug into a frown before she juts her chin and asks, "How did you get in?"

Now it's my turn to look away. She doesn't need to know that I bribed her doorman with a fully fitted—at my expense—2.0 version of Home to be let up here. "Someone was leaving as I arrived." I shrug.

I can see her trying to process my words, weighing up their truth. She must decide not to press any further because she scrubs a hand over her brow and asks, "Why are you here?"

Good question. Thinking on my feet, I reply, "We should talk about last night and what happens next."

I've never had a situation like this happen to me before, but I know Sutton enough to know that going in and demanding that she love me back isn't going to cut it. I also don't want to end up heartbroken. So, I'll play my cards close to my chest and see where she's at.

Stepping back, Sutton waves her arm for me to enter the apartment. I don't venture further than the hallway. It's important to me that she's comfortable and the fact that I've turned up on her doorstep uninvited isn't helping. She closes the door, moving to stand on the opposite side of the small table. This doesn't bode well. It's like she's putting a barrier between us and I don't like it.

With her arms folded over her chest, she shrugs. "There isn't much to talk about. We had sex, and that's it."

Rubbing a hand over my jaw, I take half a step toward her. An urgency to have her see how good together we are takes over. I should have said this a long time ago. Like four years ago. "It's not *it* for me. I want more. Last night was just the start."

Her eyes dart back and forth, searching for what, I'm not sure. "You just want something that you see as unattainable."

My response is immediate. "That's not true."

I don't miss the pleading note in her voice when she replies, "It is. For years, you could have had me and you didn't show an ounce of interest. We slept together, and I left. That's the only reason you're here now. If I'd have stayed, can you hand on heart say you wouldn't have shown me the door?"

I run a hand through my hair, desperation dragging the words from my lips as I continue, "Christ, Sutton, I— when it comes to you, I don't have any control over myself. You consume me."

Her lips part and her eyes widen, as if she can't quite believe what I'm saying. "You don't have to lie to me, Jack. And I sure as hell don't need you to protect my ego. We fucked, that's it."

Taking another step forward, I growl, "Fucked? We made love, Sutton. Tell me, has another man ever made your body come alive like that?"

She laughs, looking over into the living room and out into the city. Lifting her chin, she replies, "Yes. Another man has."

"Bullshit."

Venom laces her words when she spits, "You're best *fucking* friend, Jack. He fucked me like that, too. If not better. Face it, you lost your chance four years ago. Christ, you had a shot in college and weren't interested, so what's changed? Do you need someone with some standing in society to get you into a party or something?"

Closing the distance between us, I tilt her chin up, crushing my lips to hers. When I pull away, my voice is dangerously low as I say, "Don't you ever fucking diminish what we've shared. Or how much I want you for *you*. One day you'll see just how much you have to offer with your mind, body, and soul, not your fucking standing in society. That shit doesn't matter, okay?"

I might have harbored feelings of her being too good for me, but I went out and made something of myself so I could be the man for her. Everything I've achieved since college, in part, has been driven by a need to prove to myself that I can provide for her.

"It does matter, Jack. Why can't you see that?"

The need to show her that whatever it is that's holding her back doesn't mean shit, consumes me. Maybe if I remind her of how good we are together physically, she'll open her eyes to what we can be outside of the bedroom.

"Who said it matters?"

She turns her face away, her eyes glassy and sadness pulling at her features. "I said."

"Then you're fucking wrong. How can two people that fit together so well not be made for each other?"

With my hands cupping her face, I walk her until her back hits the wall. Heat mixed with uncertainty sparks to life in her eyes. I know she's close, but whether it's to giving in or pushing me away, I'm not sure.

Her voice is small, like she doesn't quite believe in her own words. "That's just lust and you can't build a solid foundation off of attraction."

Dipping my head, I nuzzle her neck, inhaling her floral scent. "Bullshit," I murmur.

Sutton's hands land on my biceps. I expect her to push me away but she exposes her neck to me, gripping onto my arms. Her voice is breathless as she replies, "It's true."

Don't push me away, baby. Please.

Lifting her in my arms, I press her body between mine and the wall and she wraps her legs around my waist. Her fingers dive into my hair as I lick and nip at the flesh of her collarbone.

"Name me one couple."

Dazed, she replies, "Huh?"

"For every couple you can name that got together because of their social standing, I'll name you one based on lust, attraction, or love. If you can name one and I can't, I'll walk away and drop the matter."

Her hips are gently rocking against me, but I'm not sure she even realizes. "I don't know. I... I can't think straight."

I fight the grin that threatens to break free. Licking the column of her neck, I ask, "You want a little help getting some clarity, baby?"

"Yes. Oh God, yes."

With one arm banded around her waist, I use the other to free my cock. I'm as hard as a rock and ready for her. Thank God she's wearing a dress. I might be playing a little dirty, but I need her to see what I see.

Pulling the G-string she's wearing to the side, I swipe the head of my cock through her slit. Her wetness coats me, making me groan.

Our mouths are less than an inch away when I push into her. She sucks in a breath and at the same time as I clench my teeth and hiss one out.

Without taking my eyes off of her, I thrust my hips up until I'm buried to the hilt. She's warm and wet, her walls clenching around me as she tips her head back. I have no doubt that she's trying to hide from me.

Growling, I command, "Look at me, Sutton. If you're going to have my cock buried inside of you, you're going to *fucking* look at me."

Heavy eyes meet mine as she grips onto my shoulders. I need her to see how made for each other we are. If she does, then maybe she'll stop pushing me away and we can make a go of it.

It's almost tantric, our eyes locked on each other as I move at a steady pace in and out of her. She moans, digging her fingers into my hair as she guides my head to her chest. I lick and nip at her exposed skin disappointed that she's not naked.

Later. I'll take my time and worship her body.

This is about showing her she can be herself with me. To give her a release to let go and see what I see; that we're made for each other. I keep up the pace, panting into her neck as I demand, "Tell me what you want."

"More." It's a plea, and one I want to fulfill for her.

"More of what?"

Sutton's nails dig into my shoulders through the fabric of my t-shirt. Her frustration is clear when she moans, "More of you."

"Baby, tell me how you want me."

Slowing my movements, I move one of her legs over my forearm, before doing the same to the other. The position gives me greater access, stretching her out for me to go deeper and give her more.

"Yes," she groans. "Just like that. It's so good. You fit so well. The only one who's ever fit like this"

My chest expands, blooming at her words and urging me on. We do fit so well together. Picking up the pace, I pound into her until I'm teetering on the edge.

"Fuck, baby, please tell me you're close."

Her fingers cup my face, lifting it to hers. With her mouth within touching distance, she replies, "So close. Please don't stop."

As if I stood a chance. Leaning forward, I crush my mouth to hers, devouring her. Our tongues tangle with an urgency as we race toward our climax. I feel the tension growing at the base of my spine, my balls getting heavier with each thrust.

Through clenched teeth, I demand, "Touch yourself."

Sutton moves a hand from my shoulder to under the material of her dress gathered around her waist. I want to see, but the fabric covers her from my view. It doesn't matter, there's no way in hell I'm moving. Instead, I picture her rubbing at her clit.

The clench of her walls around my cock tells me she's close. The feeling is enough to send me over. My cock pulses inside of her as I come with a ferocity that threatens to floor me. As much as I want to, I don't stop thrusting.

Her walls clench around me, strangling my cock, making me groan. Sutton digs her fingernails into my shoulders—no doubt she'll leave marks—as she cries out through her orgasm. When the tremors racking her body have subsided, she moans, "I can't take any more."

My movements stop and I pull out, my cock covered in our combined releases. Setting her down, I tuck myself back into my jeans before lifting my eyes to meet hers. My brows furrow at the closed off look in her eyes.

She pushes me away, smoothing her clothes back into place before wrapping her arms around her waist. She's shutting me out and the debutante facade is coming back. *For fuck's sake.*

Frustration bubbles in the pit of my stomach, and I run a hand through my hair. "Don't do this, Sutton. Don't shut down on me."

She ignores me, lifting her chin as she says, "If you'd have shown up at my door four years ago and asked me out..." She pauses, offering me a sad smile as she shakes her head. "Well, I would have jumped at the chance because I had feelings for you, Jack. Big, crazy, stupid feelings. Ones that overwhelmed me so much that I wasn't sure you'd have been able to handle it if I told you. I could barely deal with them myself."

I take a step forward, praying she can see how much I want her to give us a chance. "Then don't push me away. Don't stand there and tell me those feelings have gone away, Sutton."

She pulls in a breath, leaning back against the wall, her gaze unable to hold mine. Lifting her chin, I see the determination in her eyes and know I've lost her. "That's exactly what I'm telling you. They have gone, Jack. Don't ever use sex to get your way with me again. What happened just now and back in London was a mistake. I was with your best friend. The guy you were inseparable from for years. A lot of time has passed and feelings fade. It's best if we accept that we'll only ever be friends."

Crowding into her, I take hold of her chin, forcing her to look at me. "You can lie to me all you want, Sutton, but don't you dare fucking tell me that your past relationship is going to be the reason we don't have a chance. I might have fucked up once, but with all the cards on the table now, it's you putting a stop to us."

We stare at each other for the longest time. She doesn't say a word and although I want to stay and beg her to tell me she didn't mean it I don't think she'll change her mind.

Looking away, I run my fingers through my hair, defeat drowning me. There's no point in sticking around. I swing open the door, letting it close behind me as I walk away from the only woman I've ever loved.

THIRTEEN

Sutton

What have I done?

The moment the door clicks shut behind him, it's like a knife to the heart. I want to chase after him. Instead, I collapse against the wall, dropping down to the floor and wrapping my arms around my legs.

A sob gets lodged in my throat, choking me. I didn't mean a word I said. The need to protect myself from heartache had the lies spilling from my lips before I could stop them.

I guess him walking out proved my point; he was never truly in this.

On shaky legs, I stand and walk back to the living room, making a beeline for the wine glass I left on the coffee table. Snatching it up, I down the contents before collapsing back onto the couch.

A single tear runs down my cheek, but I dash it away.

The cold screen of my phone pressing against my bare thigh urges me to reach out to my friends. Holding it in my hand, I open up the screen and hesitate for a moment before pulling up the group chat.

My fingers fly across the screen, typing out a message before hovering over the send button. I can't press it, not when his sister's in the chat. Yes, she's my friend, but I don't want to make her uncomfortable.

But she won't care about that.

I know Savannah well enough to know that's true. It will be me using her as an excuse to deal with this alone when really I need my friends. With my mind made up, my thumb sends the message and I throw my phone to the side. It vibrates moments later, pulling my attention from the view in front of me. Surprisingly, Savannah is the first to message back.

SAVANNAH

First of all, never apologize for needing us. Second of all, I'm on my way.

ALEX

I'm coming too. I'll pick up wine and ice cream on the way.

After a few minutes, Meghan's name pops up and I know she's been liaising with Ben.

MEGHAN

Ben's on his way over here. Dial us in when you get there.

A smile spreads across my face before it crumples, overwhelmed by the support of my friends. How did I get so lucky to have found this group?

They find me twenty minutes later, a sobbing mess on my couch. Savannah envelopes me in a hug, her palm soothing my back as she rocks me back and forth. Alex calls Ben and Meghan, updating them before propping her phone up against the thick aesthetic books on the coffee table.

I thought I was stronger than this.

Pulling out of Savannah's arms, I wipe at my cheeks, sucking in a breath. Maybe if I think of something else, I won't keep bursting into tears. It's not like we were together, we hooked up, twice. *And then I pushed him away.*

Alex squeezes my knee, handing me a fresh glass of wine. "Whenever you're ready, we're here to listen. If you wanna just sit in silence, we can do that too."

Savannah rubs my back. "I second that."

Their words give me the courage to speak and the story tumbles from my lips as I tell them everything that's happened since college, right up until Jack left my apartment less than half an hour ago.

"What's wrong with me? He was right there, and I pushed him away, and for what, exactly? So he can find a woman that can give him something other than her family's Rolodex?" My words hang in the air with the echo of a hiccup. When I drop my eyes to my lap, I realize

I've finished my second glass of wine. *No wonder I feel tipsy.*

Ben's the first one to break through the silence that surrounds us. "That's a lot, Sutton. I'm sorry you've been dealing with this on your own. There's nothing wrong with you and it hurts me—as I'm sure it does the girls— that you sound so heartbroken. Why not reach out to him and have a conversation? No sex, just talking. Maybe make it somewhere public?"

I think about Ben's words. The sex with Jack is mind-blowing, but it's also really distracting. Being near him in general short circuits my senses. We know that we work in the bedroom—and against walls—but would we work outside of that?

Of course we would. I just need to look at our date to know that.

But was he pretending? Nothing he's said, even when I've asked him outright, has assured me that he's looking for more than a casual thing. *And yet, what did he say when he was standing in front of me earlier?*

I'm so confused.

Clearly, he was lying about something. I just don't know if it was him wanting something casual or being consumed by me.

"I have a confession to make." Savannah blushes, dropping her gaze to her lap before lifting it and rushing, "It was my idea for Jack to follow you to London. I know that he's had a thing for you ever since he came back and found me in Noah's arms. He was more upset that Noah might be cheating on you than he was about the prospect of Noah dating his sister."

I can't help the laugh that bubbles up from my lips before I sober as her declaration sinks in. My voice is urgent as I ask, "What do you mean he's had a thing for me?"

Savannah's eyes widen a fraction, but it's enough for me to know that she thinks she might have let something slip she shouldn't have. Her eyes dart over to Alex before returning to me. "Well, it was just little things you said that gave me an idea, and then when he turned up at Noah's apartment... I'm not sure I should be tellin' you all of this, Sutton. I think you should do what Ben said and go and talk to him."

Standing, I move to the window, needing some space. Today has been a lot to unpack. I want to cling to the hope that Savannah has just given me, but I know that it's not true. If Jack wanted me, he would have stayed and fought for me.

A tightness twists in my chest, and I rub over the center of it to ease the ache. Instinctively, my hand moves and I flip the pendant around my neck before wrapping an arm around my waist. Anything to hold myself together.

"Maybe I just need to sleep on it?" It comes out as more of a question than a statement. The truth is, I don't know what to do. Jack has never given me any indication —before tonight—that he might want more than a friendship or fling.

Sure, in college, when it was just the two of us, I thought there was shared looks of something *more*. But it was painfully obvious when he never acted on it that it was one-sided.

Ben's soothing voice comes through the phone and I walk back to the couch to look at him on the video call. He's always full of wisdom, but I guess that comes to him naturally, especially given his job. "It can't hurt to sleep on it. But I need you to know a couple of things because I can see how in your head you are. One, you are worthy of love and happiness. Two, anyone who has been there when the two of you are in the same room can see that he has a thing for you. Three, if you've had feelings for him for as long as you have, don't let him get away again. And four, you are a success in your own right, Sutton. There is so much you have to offer him aside from the connections your family has. Just know that we'll stand by you and cheer you on no matter the outcome, but please, you've got to at least try. Even if it scares you. *Just try*."

Tears well in my eyes at Ben's words. Of course he's right. I should at least try. If Jack rejects me, it won't break me, but at least I'll know where I stand. And I won't regret it, just like I don't regret our date. My heart races when I think about Jack taking me into his arms and telling me he feels the same way. I want nothing more than for that to be the case, but I know I'll survive if it's not.

Shaking my head, I swallow thickly before I affirm,

"I'll take a couple of days, get my thoughts together, and then go and see him."

Alex and Savannah wrap their arms around me and I offer up a watery smile to Meghan and Ben.

The corner of Meghan's mouth lifts before she says, "I'll come to the city tomorrow. Cooper has the kids, and we can go for lunch."

I make eye contact with each of them before saying, "I'd like that. Thank you guys. I can't begin to tell you how grateful I am to have you here."

Alex squeezes me into her side. "You don't need to thank us for our friendship. If any of us needed a shoulder to cry on, or for Ben to part his profound wisdom on us, we'd be there in a heartbeat. Now, let's put a movie on, get some more wine, and order food. I'm starving."

I spend the rest of the evening with Savannah and Alex, watching comedies and eating our bodyweight—or should I say Savannah does—in Thai food. At midnight, they offer to stay and sleep in the spare rooms, but I turn them down, needing the space to think through how I'm going to approach Jack.

The last thing I want is to bombard him with my feelings. But then again, subtlety hasn't gotten me very far with him up until now. One thing I know for sure is that I want to speak to him before I leave for Vegas on Friday.

FOURTEEN

Jack

I don't know what day it is and if it wasn't for the clock in the corner of the screen on the sports channel I'm watching, I wouldn't have a clue what time it was either. I've been blankly staring at the screen since I came down this morning after yet another night of fitful sleep.

Since leaving Sutton's place on Tuesday night, I've had to fight the need clawing inside of me that's desperate to return. I've gone back and forth on whether it would be a stupid idea to beg her to let me in and love me. In the early hours of one of the mornings since— with the help of my old friend *Macallan*—I decided to save my ego and wallow in my self pity until I'm finally over her. It's a solid plan.

That's never going to happen.

A pounding sounds at the door, but I ignore it.

Whoever it is can come back another day. Or never. I'm not in the mood for company.

Lifting the glass of brown liquid to my lips, I take a sip, savoring the smoky flavor. I've at least managed to wait until it's a reasonable time to start drinking each night. There's more pounding before the sound of the keypad singing out a familiar tune finally has my attention.

The door opens, and Noah stands on the threshold. *How did he even guess the new code?* This is an invasion of privacy. He doesn't find me walking into his place uninvit—okay, maybe one time, but never again. His face shows nothing as he shrugs out of his jacket, and hangs it on the hook by the door. He kicks off his shoes, walking to the kitchen without saying a word as if he lives here. My brows draw together. I know he's a man of few words but this is just weird.

When he returns to the living room, he helps himself to the whiskey on the coffee table, filling up the glass he brought in from the kitchen. I'm still staring at him when he relaxes back into the cushions.

"What are you doing? And how did you guess my new code?"

He doesn't respond, instead, he takes a sip of his drink and focuses his attention on the screen.

Fine.

If he wants to ignore me, then we can silently watch Friday night football. Because apparently it's Friday.

Fucking hell.

Three days have passed? How is that even possible?

I wonder if she's feeling anything like I am or if she's moved on and... *Oh God, what if she was seeing someone else?* No, I know Sutton. She would never have gone on a date with me, let alone slept with me, if she was seeing someone.

Noah pulls his phone out of his pocket, tapping away on the screen before he sets it on the cushion next to him. He's probably texting my sister to tell her what a sad sap I've turned into.

His words are quiet and sure, yet I know there's a whole load of anger behind them. "You know Savannah has been worried sick about you the past two days. She hasn't eaten because she's been that worked up, which is saying something. And don't even tell me she could have stopped by. She tried to, but you ignored her and changed the code."

My fingers tighten around my glass and a thickness settles in my throat. "So you just decided to ignore the massive fucking hint I was leaving? Why are you even here, Noah?"

In truth, it didn't even cross my mind to reach out to anyone and my phone's still dead. What would have been the point anyway? I take a sip of my drink, my eyes unfocused on the TV in front of me.

"Do you want my opinion?"

Noah's question forces me to look at him. My gaze searches his face. I find nothing but compassion and a friendship that's lasted fifteen years without so much as a bad word said between us.

Taking a sip of my whiskey, I come up short, finding the glass empty. I push it onto the table in front of me before leaning back and resting my head on the back of the couch. "I'm sure you're going to tell me anyway."

Noah puts his glass on the table before turning his body to face me. I refuse to face him. Despite having seen him at his worst, I'm not sure I want to show him mine. Sure, he saw my grief when my dad died, but even then I kept how broken I was to myself.

Except with her.

The memory of Sutton finding me in tears in my dorm room all those years ago plays behind my eyes like a movie. She held me in her arms, our night of studying long forgotten as she comforted me. I still remember the feel of her fingers combing through my hair as she held me against her chest and murmured words I don't remember.

Blinking, I force the images away and focus on the present. There's no point in searching the past for signs of something that was never there. No matter how much I wish I could go back and tell her how I feel, I don't have a time machine.

Maybe I can make one.

That's a stupid idea. I'd only be making one to end up heartbroken again.

Noah's voice cuts through my crazy thoughts. "I think, if you truly love her—which it's pretty obvious you do, given the code to get into your apartment is her fucking birthday dude—then don't let her get away." He pauses, running his hand down the front of his t-shirt. "Do you know what my biggest regret in life is?"

I shake my head, even though I have some idea given he let me know just how mad he was that we didn't communicate properly. I'll hold my hands up. Noah and my sister not being together is totally my fault. If I'd been clearer with him on the promise I made him make me, then he wouldn't have spent all that time trying to stay away from her.

A shiver runs down my spine and I gag at the thought of my best friend and little sister hooking up. I know he loves her, and I have faith that he'll treat her right, but I'm still not used to it.

Noah continues, "It was the fact that I walked away from Van the night you and I crashed Wilkins' party, and again at the party we threw in your old loft when you walked in on us. I wish I'd been man enough to tell her how I felt, because had you not called me last year, I could have lost her forever. Don't just walk away, Jack. If you love Sutton, go to her and tell her."

My breath leaves me in a huff. "I already told her."

"You outright told her you loved her?"

Well, no. "Something like that."

Picking up his glass, he lifts it to his mouth, mumbling, "You're a jackass."

"Fine, I didn't say the *exact* words. I implied them. And then she told me her feelings had died and that what we did was a mistake. Why would I lay my cards on the table after that, Noah?"

Noah looks at me like I don't have an IQ high enough to get into Mensa if I wanted to.

"Because you love her, and that's what people do. They lay themselves bare and tell the person they love that they love them. There are no guarantees in life, Jack."

Looking back at the TV, with a shrug, I reply, "I guess we'll have to agree to disagree."

"You're a fucking idiot."

"You know, you can leave if you want. Nobody's making you stay."

Noah clears his throat, replying, "Well, that's where you're wrong. I'm not allowed to go home until you agree to go to Sutton."

Standing, I walk to the kitchen needing to get away from him before I say something I might regret to my new roommate.

His voice follows me as he calls, "She's apparently as broken up about all of this as you are. I think you've both been trying to protect yourself and an honest conversation will clear everything up."

Standing in the doorway, I say, "I've always known she's out of my league, man. I was a fool to think that our friendship could be the foundation for more and that she'd give us a shot."

Noah turns to look at me over the back of the couch. "Are you serious?"

Uncertainty fills my voice. "Yeah."

"What exactly makes her out of your league? And by the way, I hate that mentality."

"She grew up rich, and I grew up poor."

Noah shakes his head, huffing out a laugh. "Absolute jackass. How many zeros are in your bank account right now?"

I'm not telling him that. It's a shit ton, but still. "What's your point?"

"My point is, you're a billionaire, Jack. If you wanted to, you could buy her a small country. This isn't about money or how either of you grew up. Just look at Grace Kelly and the Prince of Monaco."

Jesus, what has Savannah turned him into? "She was a movie star, not exactly poor."

What has she turned me into?

"But it still works. She wasn't royalty before they got married. Yes, you and Sutton had different upbringings, but she's not the type of person to even consider taking that into account. She fucking dated me and your upbringing was much better than mine. Stop being a pussy and go and get her, so I can go home."

Busying myself in the kitchen, I replay Noah's words. *Is he right? Am I making a mistake by walking away?*

FIFTEEN

Sutton

The sharp, stabbing pain that's been in my chest since the moment he left my apartment is still there. Are you supposed to feel physical pain from heartbreak? Maybe I should go to the ER. Just to get checked out.

It's better to be safe than sorry, as Minnie likes to say. Although she's usually talking about wearing condoms and having an IUD, it applies in other circumstances. Especially because I can't have a broken heart. We were never together officially, so it's not possible.

But why have I barely showered in the four days since he left?

Why did I cancel important meetings because I couldn't bear to leave my apartment and put on a happy face?

Grabbing a pillow, I scream into it, feeling only marginally better. Today is the day I stop feeling sorry for myself. I'm going to shower, put some makeup on, my favorite outfit, and then I'm going to his apartment. Ben was right when he said we should talk and, if nothing else, I want to either figure shit out or get my friend back. Most importantly, I want to stop feeling like this.

I go through the motions of showering and doing my hair and makeup. The entire time, my mind is preoccupied with thoughts of *how* to start the conversation. Starting it by telling him I love him is probably too much. Or is it? No, it definitely is. Especially given how we left it.

My phone buzzes from its place on my bedside table. With the black summer mini dress I'm going to wear over my arm, I walk out of the closet and lay it on the bed. Swiping up my phone, I freeze the moment my eyes land on his name.

JACK

Are you home?

My brows furrow as I re-read his message.

SUTTON

Yes.

JACK

Good. Come downstairs.

What is going on? My fingers fly across the screen, hope blossoming in my chest.

SUTTON

You're here?

His response is almost immediate.

JACK

Please, Sutton, come downstairs.

Why is he here?

What does it matter? He's *here*. Jack has come to me, and I'll be damned if I don't go to him. I'm walking toward the door before I realize I'm only in my robe. Spinning around, I grab my dress, throw it on, and stop in front of the mirror by the bedroom door.

My cheeks are slightly flushed and excitement dances behind my eyes. One of two things is going to happen. Either he's here to get our friendship back on track or... I don't even want to think about what the 'or' could mean.

Fluffing up my hair, I walk back into my closet, grabbing up a pair of black heels before heading for the door. My eyes go to the window in the living room. Drizzle slides down the pane, obscuring the view I've spent many nights alone looking at. *Thank God, it should start to get cooler now*. I freeze with one hand on the doorknob as I'm transported back to the night that started it all.

Did it though?

I guess not. My feelings for Jack took root from the moment my eyes landed on him in our communications class. They've always been there. It's just that for brief periods of time, I've pushed them into the shadows, hiding them from my conscious mind.

That ends today.

Whether he likes it or not.

The only thing I have to offer Jack is my love, and that has to count for something. It has to be *enough*. Pulling open the door, I move with purpose toward the elevator. I jab the button and tap my foot with a mixture of impatience and nerves as I wait.

It feels like a lifetime before it arrives and then begins its descent to the lobby. The entire time, I run over what I want to say; how I want to express my love for him. Hurried and with excitement? Slow and with trepidation? I settle on steady and with determination. It's not like I don't know this man. He's been my friend for nearly fourteen years and never once has he made me feel like I couldn't express myself to him. I put those limitations on myself.

The doors slide open, and as I step out, my eyes coast across the space. *He's not here.* The pain in my chest comes back with a vengeance. It's only at this moment that I realize it never went away.

One last look around the near-empty lobby halts me when I see Jack's blurry figure on the other side of the glass, standing in the rain. My hand goes to my stomach, as the tension in my body releases. Each step feels like it's happening in slow motion as I walk toward him, trying not to race across the space.

With trembling hands I push through the door, leaning out slightly as I call over the sounds of the city, "What are you doing?"

Rocking back on his heels, his hands stuffed in his pockets, he shouts, "Come here."

I hesitate, the desire to keep myself looking half-decent nearly winning out. The smile on his face calls to me, daring me to live on the edge. I'm walking forward, out into the rain, before I can question the idea. My once floaty dress clings to my thighs, the fabric getting heavier the longer I'm outside.

Coming to a stop in front of Jack, I look up at him at a loss for words. He looks tired and there's a sadness behind his eyes that has worry gnawing at my gut.

Hesitation laces his words when he asks, "Can I have this dance?"

He holds out his hand and I stare at it, confused for a moment. "Why?"

"Because I have some things to say and it's easier to do when I'm not looking directly at you."

My head snaps back, hurt by his words. I take a step away from him, suddenly feeling very mentally unprepared for this conversation.

Seeing the effect his words have had on me, Jack scrubs a hand over the back of his neck before saying, "Christ, not in a bad way. Just... Please, can I have this dance?"

I want to ask him why again, but he probably won't tell me, and giving him this one dance will give me the answer. Placing my hand in his, I allow him to wrap an arm around my waist as he steps into my space. The clean citrus smell that's all him invades my senses. I close my eyes and straighten my spine in an attempt to hide from him—and in a way myself.

Jack's voice is a deep rumble against my chest when he speaks. "You can relax. It's just me."

Blowing out a breath, I give a humorless laugh when I say, "That's the problem."

He dips his head, resting his cheek on the top of my head. "I'm sorry for leaving on Tuesday. And for taking so long to come and see you. I've been processing a lot but mostly just feeling like crap for how we left things."

In the middle of a New York sidewalk, under the light drizzle of rain, he continues to sway us to the music that is unique to the city. "Even now, I don't know how exactly to say what I want to. What I need to say to you and should have a long time ago. Do you remember the day we met?"

I want to lift my head and look into his eyes, but I'm afraid of what I might find because I want nothing more than to see him craving me as much as I do him. Instead, I settle for nodding and wait for him to continue.

"When I saw you that day, I thought, 'she's so beautiful and definitely way out of my league'. Christ, you looked like you belonged in a museum. Not a hair out of place and dressed in an outfit that I'm certain cost more than my entire wardrobe. I was determined to keep to myself and just admire you from afar, but you came and sat next to me. And the second you did, I was fucking gone."

This time I do look up. His focus is on the building

behind me, but the ticking of the muscle in his jaw tells me how worried he is about what he's saying. I'm almost afraid to speak because I don't want to stop him from telling me what he's feeling.

"You were so buttoned up and yet I loved seeing you open up for me as time went on. But it got to a point where I wasn't sure you'd ever see me as anything more than a friend. Especially when I saw how you were with other guys you dated. I resigned myself to being the guy who was in love with you but could never have you.

"Jesus, I come from a family of people who didn't have two dimes to rub together at some points. I thought I could never give you what you wanted or needed, so I worked damn hard to get there. To be the man that was good enough for you and yet I still held myself back, because I didn't know if I could be enough."

Sunshine peeks through the buildings behind him as he looks down. His mouth is open slightly as he holds eye contact with me. There's a hopefulness in his gaze and it has a fluttering erupting in my stomach.

He's baring himself to me. And yet, the words that form in my mind and the ones that spill from my lips are not the same. "Why didn't you tell me this when I asked you why you wanted to go on a date with me?"

I go to step out of his arms, to put some distance between us, but his hold on my waist tightens before he drops his forehead to mine. "Don't put the shutters down, Sutton. *Please*."

The pleading in that single word has my body

relaxing back into his. I'll hear him out because I still need answers. Even if being in his arms is clouding my judgment. *I just need to be strong.*

There's a raspiness to his voice that sends a shiver down my spine when he speaks. "I didn't tell you because I wasn't sure you'd be able to handle my *true* reasons. I'm not putting my cowardice on you, but you'd never given me any indication that you felt anything but friendship for me. I'd rather have you in my life as a friend than not at all, even if it kills me to see you move on and be happy with someone else."

"So, why are you telling me now?"

"Because I'm tired of living with my regrets. You told me that you had feelings for me once and I don't think they can be switched off, despite what you said. I'm hoping that there's a small part of you that still wants me."

I don't want to be hopeful when he hasn't said what I need him to. But with the rain having stopped and the warm summer sun drying us, I can't help but feel like everything might be okay. It might work out.

His gaze is questioning, a groove appearing between his eyes. It's only now, as he's waiting for my answer, that I realize we've come to a stop. My tongue darts out, nervously swiping over my lips.

Pushing out of his arms, I scrub a hand over my forehead, trying to get my thoughts to focus. "I don't understand. Why now, Jack? After all this time, you're saying that you have feelings for me and yet you didn't stay and fight for me."

He steps forward, his hand reaching out for me before dropping away. "I know and I'm sorry."

"Sorry doesn't fix it. I've loved you for thirteen years and you've never once shown any sign of interest. You can't stand there and tell me that you now want me and expect me to just say 'okay, that's great'."

His voice is loud, drawing attention when he replies, "Don't you think I know that? Fucking hell, Sutton." Jack runs a frustrated hand through his hair, tugging on the strands. "You want me to list out all the things I love about you? Fine. I love that you play with the chain around your neck when you're unsure and nervous. I love your scent and the way your eyes sparkle when you're having fun.

"And that you're too fucking polite. Case in point, despite knowing it would make you ill, you still ate the shellfish Stacey Woods served at our graduation party because nobody else would touch it and you didn't want her to be upset. I love that you've built a business from the ground up and you're thriving with it. I'm so fucking proud of you for that, baby. I love how you let your guard down and can be yourself around me when you want to. I love how you stole my t-shirt when you ran out on me. It was my favorite, by the way."

I can't hold back the smile that spreads across my face or the tears of happiness that roll down my cheeks.

Jack moves forward, cupping my face. "Don't cry, baby. You can keep it."

"I will, thank you. But these are happy tears."

He grins before his face sobers and becomes serious. "There are so many more things I love about you, but there's one thing I love most. You make me feel invincible, like I can get through anything, as long as I have you. That day you found me in my dorm was the worst day of my life, Sutton. But you held me and you fixed me, just by being you."

My fingers grip the fabric at the waist of his damp t-shirt, anchoring myself. I pull in a deep breath, forcing the words from my lips. "You weren't the only one who wasn't brave enough to say how they felt. I could have told you how much I wanted you too. Self preservation is the only thing that made me send you away on Tuesday. God, I wanted you to stay so bad.

"I've been all up in my own head ever since I walked into that classroom thirteen years ago. I've been telling myself that I could never keep up with you. You were always such a brilliant overachiever and I... well, I wasn't. I always knew you were going to make something of yourself, so what could I have possibly offered a guy like you?" My voice cracks on the question.

His tone is fierce as he says, "So fucking much, baby. Don't ever think like that again. Do you hear me?"

I nod, tears welling in my eyes. Of course I already know that now, but it feels good to have him tell me.

Jack dusts a kiss over the apple of my cheek before

moving to the next. His lips dust gentle kisses around my face, not touching my mouth as he says, "That's my girl. I love you, Sutton, and I'm sorry for not telling you sooner."

He doesn't give me the opportunity to say it back as he captures my lips in a searing kiss that has my knees going weak. When we come up for air, I tuck my face into the space between his collarbone and jaw, not bothering to conceal the grin spreading across my face, even when my cheeks ache.

Jack pulls me into his arms, humming a song as we sway on the sidewalk. Resting my head on his shoulder, I ask, "What's this one called?"

He pauses, dusting his lips over my forehead before he replies, "*Wondering Why* by The Red Clay Stays."

This time, instead of continuing to hum the tune, he whispers the words to me. It's a story about a man and woman from different backgrounds and how he's bewildered by her love for him. If he hadn't told me this was a song, I would have thought it was about us.

Lifting my head, I snag Jack's lips, wrapping my arms around his neck as we continue to move. We're lost in our own little world until I pull away and murmur, "I love you."

His mouth stretches across his face and a light shines bright in his eyes. There's a wonder in his voice when he replies, "I love you too."

Biting my bottom lip, I look up at him under my

eyelashes. "How about you take me inside and warm me up?"

He wiggles his brows, a mischievous smile on his lips. "With pleasure."

I don't expect it when he swoops me up into his arms, but I take the opportunity to snuggle into him and tell him—in explicit detail—all the ways I'm going to make up for the years we missed being together.

Epiloque - Sutton

THREE MONTHS LATER

Nerves have taken up residence in the pit of my stomach, and I don't have a clue why. Well, that's not strictly true. Tonight is the first night Jack and I are going to see Noah and Savannah alone since we became a couple. It's not like I haven't spent time with Savannah and Noah before. I mean, I lived with them for months when Noah and I dated.

Who am I kidding?

This isn't a dynamic that you come across every day.

My hand shakes as I drag my brush through my hair. Maybe if I stay in the bathroom, we won't have to go. I could lock the door and then Jack would either have to go by himself or stay here with me. Even better, I could say the lock broke and I can't get out.

Jack walks into the room, pulling me from my planning and ruining any ideas I might have that involve locking myself in. "Are you ready?"

Putting my brush on the counter, I face him, leaning back against the unit. My words are rushed and kind of desperate. "Do I have to go?"

He chuckles, coming to stand in front of me. His hands land on my hips, before dipping lower and under the hem of my silk robe. My breath hitches as it does every time he touches me. It's an effort to keep my head from tipping back and losing myself in the sparks that zing through me.

Jack's voice is low and dangerous when he asks, "What's wrong?"

He traces little circles over my bare thigh as his hand moves up and onto my hip. I have no doubt he knows what he's doing.

My voice is breathless and aroused when I reply, "I'm nervous."

Completely unfazed by the storm of desire he's stirring inside of me, Jack asks, "Why are you nervous?"

Widening my stance, I silently beg for his hand to move closer to my clit. Thoughts are not coming, aside from the one screaming at him to relieve me.

His hand traces over the skin of my hip, teetering closer to the apex of my thighs. A whimper slips free and I blink up at him.

"Why are you nervous?"

Right. Get back on track. "It's a different dynamic. I'd rather stay home with you."

I moved into Jack's brownstone a little over a month ago. At dinner six weeks ago, we had a talk about the timeline of our relationship and where we're going. That weekend, I moved all of my stuff in.

The first time I woke up to an empty bed at three in the morning was an eventful night. It took me twenty minutes of searching the house before I found his note telling me he was in his lab in the basement.

Jack's hand falls away from under my robe. It's on the tip of my tongue to beg him but he drops to his knees and asks, "Would it help if I gave you a distraction?"

Nodding, I keep my eyes trained on him as he unties the belt, making the sides of my robe fall open. He buries his nose between my legs, rubbing it back and forth over the lacy material. The contact on my clit has my eyes closing and my head tipping back. He makes light work of removing my G-string before lifting one leg over his shoulder.

My fingers grip the counter for balance as my moans echo around the bathroom and he swipes his tongue through my pussy from the entrance to my clit. His tongue is hypnotic, flicking at my clit before dipping into me. The vibrations are nearly too much.

Rocking my hips, I grip Jack's hair, guiding him to where I need him most. He presses a finger into me, stretching my walls as he devours my pussy. The sound of his finger moving in and out is amplified in the acoustics of the bathroom.

Forcing my eyes down, I look at Jack on his knees, savoring my taste. It's my favorite sight. That and when I'm sitting on his face and I can see the heat in his eyes.

My hand lifts to my breast, rolling the nipple between my fingers as I focus on my own pleasure.

"That's it, baby. Ride my face and fingers."

He adds another finger, increasing his pace and pressure. *It's too much.* Despite my desire to hold back, my legs go numb as the pleasure takes over me. Spasms wrack my body, threatening to send me falling to the floor. It's almost embarrassing how quickly he can bring me to orgasm.

Jack presses a hand into my chest, keeping me upright. I'm still coming down from the incredible high he's taken me to when he stands, wrapping an arm around my waist.

"Still nervous?"

Words won't form, so I shake my head. I'm not nervous anymore but it doesn't mean I can function like a normal human being. My breaths come in short sharp pants and I cling to his shirt.

"Good. Think you can finish getting ready?"

My voice comes out as a croak. "Yes."

Bending his knees, Jack holds my gaze, smoothing my hair back from my face as he says, "I love you. You're a strong, capable woman and those nerves you felt are the good kind. The ones that come from being excited about what's to come. Just remember that."

"I love you too."

So much.

But it doesn't mean I want to go.

Jack laughs, rubbing his thumb over my lips. "Stop pouting."

"Fine. But only because you'll owe me when we get home."

His eyebrows lift. "I think you'll find it's you that owes me."

Shrugging a shoulder I turn in his arms, facing the mirror and running my fingers through my hair. "We'll see about that."

He slaps me on the ass before walking out of the bathroom and calling, "We certainly will."

As much as I believe that everything happens for a reason and that things work out the way they're supposed to, I can't help but be a little regretful when it comes to Jack and I not having figured things out sooner.

The only saving grace is all the years we have to come. I can't wait to see where the ride takes us, but I know it'll be fun and eventful because I'm with him.

The End

Afterword

Thank you so much for reading my One Date. If you loved Sutton and Jack's story, be sure to leave a review.

Be sure to sign up to my newsletter here (subscribepage.io/4kdNEJ) and get monthly updates on my books, enter giveaways and hear about some other awesome authors.

Want to find out how Meghan and Cooper met, what caused Alex to hate Sebastian or all about that promise Noah made to Jack? You can find the Breaking the Rules series here and dive right into their stories.

Acknowledgments

My thank you's always go to the same people but without these people, I wouldn't be bringing you this book.

A huge thank you, first and foremost, to Allie Bliss, my editor. I love working with you and can't wait to see what comes next. I have you to thank for how far I've come with my writing in the last year or so.

Thank you to Sarah from Word Emporium for your thorough work with proofreading One Date. You've done an amazing job, as always.

Jasmine, my PA, thank you for sticking around. Sorry I'm still a pain...I don't see that changing any time soon!

Tee, your words of wisdom are always there whenever I'm doubting myself. Thank you for having somewhere for me to ask questions, hyping up my fellow cygnets and being an inspiration of what can be achieved if you work hard enough for it.

As always a special shoutout to my street team. Every single one of you means so much to me and I hope that you stick around for all the book boyfriends that are yet to come.

Finally, a huge thank you to my boyfriend Ryan and our dog, Mia. I love you both so much.

About the Author

KA James is an author of contemporary romance. She lives near London, UK with her partner and their Bichon Frisé, called Mia. Before starting her author journey, KA was an avid reader of romance books and truly believes the spicier the book, the better.

Outside of writing, KA has worked in HR for eleven years but has truly found her passion with writing and getting lost in a world that plays out like a movie in her mind. After all, getting lost in the land of make believe, where it's much spicier is way more fun.

 KA is always in the process of writing the next book, but hopes that you enjoyed reading this one. Be sure to follow along on one or more social media channels to be kept in the loop.

Printed in Great Britain
by Amazon

52745911R10088